The Lady Grace
Mysteries

From the Daybookes
of Lady Grace Cavendish

Book the Third

Conspiracy

The Lady Grace Mysteries from Delacorte Press

ASSASSIN
BETRAYAL
CONSPIRACY

THE
Lady
Grace
MYSTERIES

*From the Daybookes
of Lady Grace Cavendish*

BOOK THE THIRD

CONSPIRACY

Patricia Finney is writing as Grace Cavendish

Published by
Delacorte Press
an imprint of
Random House Children's Books
a division of Random House, Inc.
New York

Series created by Working Partners Ltd.
Text copyright © 2005 by Working Partners Ltd.

The trademark Delacorte Press is registered in the U.S. Patent and Trademark
Office and in other countries.

Visit us on the Web! www.randomhouse.com/kids
Educators and librarians, for a variety of teaching tools, visit us at
www.randomhouse.com/teachers

Library of Congress Cataloging-in-Publication Data is available upon request.

ISBN 0-385-73153-1 (trade) — ISBN 0-385-90191-7 (GLB)
The text of this book is set in 13-point Cloister.
Book design by Trish Parcell Watts
Printed in the United States of America
February 2005
10 9 8 7 6 5 4 3 2 1
BVG

To Ben and Teazle—my family

VERY SECRETE!

DAYBOOKE THE THIRD OF

MY LADY GRACE CAVENDISH,

MAID OF HONOUR TO HER GRACIOUS MAJESTY

QUEEN ELIZABETH I OF THAT NAME

AT THE QUEEN'S COURT

ON PROGRESS

Conspiracy

*At Baron Oxey his house, in the
County of Oxfordshire
shortly before sunrise*

We are just making ready to leave Oxey Hall.
And here have I another daybooke and five fine new
quill pens from the feathers of one of the geese, and
the Queen has given me a new bottle full of ink,
made with crystal and chased with gold, and it has a
stopper that locks. She gave it me on condition I do
no more writing when wearing my white damask
gown. Not even if I am very careful. We have
unpicked the piece that somehow got ink upon it
and put a new piece of white damask in—I think it
looks very well, though Mrs. Champernowne grum-
bled that the colour was a little different.

I am writing this as I sit upon a big chest full of

clothes, wearing my black wool kirtle, which will take no harm from ink at all, so fie on you, Mrs. Champernowne.

Olwen, Lady Sarah's tiring woman, is trying to pack all Sarah's little pots of face paint and unguents, but Lady Sarah keeps unpacking them again. She has a new spot on her chin, and she is searching for an ointment her mother gave her yestereven—of goose fat with a burnt mouse's tail mixed in it—sovereign against all blemishes.

Mary Shelton is nibbling at some gingerbread and watching. "Did you never think that perhaps it is all the creams and elixirs you use that give you so many spots, Sarah?" she just asked.

Sarah only tossed her head and made a "*Ptah!*" noise, though I think Mary has a point.

When we leave the Oxeys' house, the Court will move to Kenilworth, which is my lord the Earl of Leicester's chief residence—the Queen gave it him five years ago. It is very exciting—my lord of Leicester is Master of the Queen's Horse and her best friend and he organizes all the revels and processions and ceremonies for the Court and so we are looking forward to wonderful entertainments at his own residence. My tumbler friend Masou will be performing. He has already gone ahead to make ready.

I love being on progress. Although it is tiresome to have to share a chamber with all five of the other Maids of Honour. Lady Sarah constantly fusses over her face paint—of course, I am used to that—and bickers with Lady Jane Coningsby. Carmina Willoughby and Penelope Knollys gossip incessantly like noisy geese. And Mary Shelton, with whom I share a bed, snores most horribly and keeps me awake half the night. Nevertheless, even if it were not a way for the Queen to see her people, feed the Court at the expense of her nobles, and allow the London palaces to be cleaned and whitewashed, going on progress would still be the finest way to spend the hot summer months when London is full of plague.

I don't even mind all the riding from one house to another with the rest of the Court cavalcade, because all of us Maids of Honour ride nice steady amblers and we each sit behind a groom on pillion seats. Lady Jane Coningsby, who is a good rider, complains that it is too tedious for words, but I feel much better with another controlling the horse. Somehow, whatever I ask a horse to do, I find it always does the opposite.

The Queen says I am too soft with my horse and do not make it obey me, and that is why my mounts always act so froward and unseat me—or run away with me!

Lady Sarah is now squinting to put on her spot cream by the light of one small candle. As her creams usually do, it smells very nasty despite having heal-all pounded into it as well as the mouse-tail ashes.

My dear friend Ellie, the laundrymaid, just went by with her arms full of sheets and rolled her eyes at me over Sarah. One of the best things about being on progress is that I can borrow Ellie from the laundry and have her with me as my unofficial tiring woman. She is currently making herself useful by helping Olwen pile the sheets into chests, while Olwen mutters to herself, "Wherefore six sheets and nine smocks and every one of them used? Ah, bless you, Ellie, they can all pack here, look you, and then we shall have space for the pillowcases. . . ."

One of the men from the Removing Wardrobe of Beds has begun to take down the bed curtains. Usually they wait until we are all gone but they want to be off soon. The Removing Wardrobe has two sets of everything, so while we are in Kenilworth they will be going to our next destination and setting everything up again ready for the Queen.

Now the other two men are on ladders, unpegging

the tester-frame and the posts, and carrying bed parts through the passageways and out into the courtyard. I can see the carts waiting by torchlight, with the horses still munching in their nosebags and stamping their huge hairy feet.

The Queen's Chambers are the last to go. The men always wait until she is gone before they start dismantling them and taking down the frames of brocade from the walls. When everything is ready we will go and attend upon her. Oh, no, not again! Sarah picked up another pot—with ground talcum in it this time—and a swansdown puff to carefully powder the end of her nose.

"Will you kindly be giving me that, my lady?" Olwen snapped, picking up the pot and holding her hand out for the puff. "You shall be late for attending upon Her Majesty, look you. . . ."

"But my nose is all shiny again," Sarah said with a pout. "I'll just—"

Olwen has just tutted and nipped the swansdown puff out of Sarah's fingers, because Mrs. Champernowne, Mistress of the Maids, has come bustling in.

"Where are the Maids of Honour?" she is saying. "Come along with you, now. You should have been ready to attend Her Majesty ten minutes ago!"

And so I must put my beautiful new daybooke and my penner away in my embroidery bag to attend the Queen—I wonder what she will be like today. She hates mornings but she loves progresses, so it is like tossing a coin.

Later, about noon upon the same day

We have now stopped for dinner at a gentleman's manor house, near the village of Charlecote. The gentleman who owns the house is making a speech at the moment, which is full of Latin and Greek and immensely boring. The Queen can sit and smile and look attentive for hours on end, but I can only survive by pretending to make notes on the speech, as I am doing now, while actually writing in my daybooke instead.

Luckily, the food is delicious. The Queen's cooks prepared it, and there are spit-roasted ducks in a plum sauce and kidneys in penny-loaves—and strawberries and raspberries, too! Late ones—with cream. I love them. I was going to save a few for Ellie but I couldn't bear it any more and I ate them all up.

We left Oxey Hall so early the sun was just coming up, and we rode through the cool of the morning, which was quite pleasant. My ambler, Ginger, was very well-behaved for Mr. Helston, my groom. The seat was padded, so I could sit quite comfortably and watch the fields go past—all golden with stubble after the harvest, with haystacks, fat like giant harvest mice, hunched in the corners of the fields. My groom is ancient—at least forty-five—and he talks mainly to the horse and just says, "Yes, my lady," and "No, my lady," to me. He sounds as if he has a cold.

We always ride in the same order. Mr. Hatton, the Captain of the Queen's Guard, and his men go at the front, after the harbingers and heralds. And then comes the Queen, riding her beautiful dappled grey horse that came from Hungary, and attended by the Earl of Leicester. He is her Master of Horse, so he is always by her side on progress—and besides, he is her favourite, as everyone knows. Behind and around the Queen ride the various gentlemen she likes to attend on her, followed by us Maids of Honour and all the rest of the Court.

When we passed through villages, the people came running in from the fields and the women brought their children out in their Sunday clothes. They were waiting by the road to cheer the Queen as she rode by. They were full of excitement and pride that she had chosen their village to ride through, and not the all but identical hamlet a mile away, their bitter rivals since the Romans left.

They stared at the Queen and all of us and talked about us as if we couldn't hear, which can be embarrassing: one woman tutted and said, "Well, she'm a fair maid with her red velvet hood, but from her face she's got powerful indigestion. Looks as if she swallowed a pint of vinegar!" The only one with a red hood was Lady Jane Coningsby. Lady Sarah giggled at that—she hates Lady Jane, who is not terribly popular with any of us.

The Queen is very clever and charming with her subjects and the people love her. When she spotted a baby in his shirt, squealing and waving his little biggin cap, she reined in her horse and the Earl called the halt, looking wary. It certainly was a very sweet baby. He had bright gold hair and big blue eyes and only a little snot on his upper lip. He was looking up at the Queen and roaring with laughter, I think because of all her bright sparkling jewels.

The Queen smiled down at the baby and his mother, who was flushed with pride. He crowed and started clapping, but it looked as if he had only just learned to clap because sometimes he missed and smacked his nose, which made us all smile.

"There's a fair, bold babe," the Queen said, still smiling.

His mother curtsied and held him up to her as high as she could. "And a true liegeman of Your Majesty," she puffed. "I pray God to bless you with as fine a little lad as he."

Some of the gentlemen sucked air in at that, for usually talk of babies makes the Queen sad or angry—perchance because some say that, at almost thirty-six, the Queen will soon be too old to have babes of her own, and she doesn't like to be reminded. This time she leaned down to stroke the baby's cheek. He smiled sunnily up at her and grabbed a pearl sewn to her sleeve, which came off in his hand.

"Oh, now! Look what you did, you naughty—" tutted his mother.

"Let him have the pearl," said the Queen lightly. "As a keepsake. You are a lucky woman."

The mother curtsied as the Queen rode on, and the Earl commanded us to proceed. I looked back as we went round a bend in the road, to see the mother firmly stopping the baby from putting the Queen's pearl in his mouth.

Mary Shelton, who was riding beside me, sitting pillion behind her own groom, had stopped knitting—a coat for one of her older sister's children—to watch the spectacle. She had a knowing smile on her face.

"What?" I asked.

"Mayhap the Queen is broody," she observed. "Do you think she is thinking about marriage again? She always goes broody when she does that."

I peered at the Queen ahead of us. The Earl of Leicester was leaning over slightly to listen to what she was saying to him. He normally looks disagreeable and he isn't at all popular at Court, but whenever he is near the Queen, his face softens. It's always hard to imagine people as old as the Queen and the Earl of Leicester being romantic or in love. But they have been for a long time—and I saw it quite early on, even though I didn't really understand it at the time, as I was only a small child.

Mary stared thoughtfully at me. "You must know something of Her Majesty's fondness for the Earl, Grace," she said.

I nodded. "But I was very young then—only five and just out of leading strings. I remember seeing the Queen very happy. And my mother—who as you know was one of her Ladies-in-Waiting and her closest friend—was happy for her. But worried for her, too. Because the Earl—who was not yet Earl of Leicester, and known as Robert Dudley—was already married to Amy Robsart."

"Oh, yes," said Mary eagerly. "And then Amy died, and *how* she died caused a great scandal, did it not?" she asked.

The other Maids of Honour were pretending they weren't interested, but I noticed that they had all got their grooms to ride a bit closer to listen, because of course I am the only one of us who was at Court when the scandal occurred.

I began to tell Mary what I knew of that time, eight years ago, when the Queen and Robert Dudley were first thought to be in love. My mother had told me that Her Majesty had become friends with Dudley when they were both much younger and imprisoned in the Tower of London. Queen Elizabeth was only a Princess then and she had been imprisoned by her own older sister, Mary, who was Queen at the time.

Once the Princess Elizabeth had become Queen, she and Dudley were together all the time. Whenever he jousted he wore the Queen's favour on his shoulder—her glove or kerchief—and there was lots of gossip about it. All the other nobles at Court were furious because the Dudleys were seen as a family of upstarts—and Robert Dudley's father and grandfather had both been executed for treason.

But Her Majesty didn't care—she was in love. She believed that if she waited, Dudley would be hers—because Amy Robsart was sickly and bedridden. It was only a matter of time before Dudley would be free to marry again.

"And then news came that Amy Robsart was dead," I went on. "It was said she fell and broke her neck from tripping on the stairs—"

"She tripped?" Mary said, looking doubtful. "Though she was bedridden?"

"Exactly," I said. "It was too convenient. Everyone said Dudley must have lost patience and murdered Amy to clear his way to Her Majesty. And of course such gossip meant Her Majesty had to shun Dudley—she could not be involved in a scandal. The other nobles would have been outraged. She might have lost her throne."

I didn't tell Mary what else I remembered: my mother clasping the Queen to her as Her Majesty had sobbed brokenly, whispering, "He would never do such a thing, never! But God help us, Margaret—there is no way for us to prove it!"

"No, Your Majesty," my mother had agreed sadly.

My nurse had then been sent for to take me away to pick flowers.

I turned back to Mary. "I don't know what to think. And my mother would never talk of it afterwards." And now she is dead from saving the Queen's life by accidentally drinking poison meant for her, so I can never ask her. Though I suspect she did not like Robert Dudley, and only countenanced him because the Queen was smitten and could see no wrong in him.

Talk of my mother makes me sad, for I miss her terribly. Although, since her tragic death just over a year ago, the Queen has been very kind to me and has quite taken me under her wing. Indeed, that is why I am her Maid of Honour, even though I am so young.

While Mary and I were talking about this, we could see the Earl of Leicester riding ahead in the cavalcade with the Queen. He is quite handsome and tall, with flashing blue eyes and dark hair, and he is a wonderful horseman. Of course he is very old—one year older than the Queen, and I think he is getting a bit heavy. He is arrogant and ill-tempered, except when he talks to the Queen—and then he is charming and patient, even when Her Majesty is cross with him and hits him with her fan.

I wonder if he really did murder his wife. If I had been a Lady Pursuivant for the Queen then—in charge of pursuing and apprehending all wrongdoers at Court—as I am now, perhaps I could have found out the truth of it. . . .

We couldn't talk any more about it, because we had arrived at this little village with its small manor house, where I am writing now. The gentleman is *still* speechifying to the Queen, but when he has stopped and the Queen has finished dinner, we will head on to Kenilworth and— Oh, good! I think the speech is coming to an end.

A few moments later

Hell's teeth! The speech *did* stop for a little and we all sighed with relief, but then the gentleman drank a toast to the Queen and started again! How does he remember it all? At least I have just had a very interesting conversation with Mary Shelton.

"The Queen is up to something—there's a plot afoot," Mary said to me quietly, with her mouth full. "Did you hear that there will be a new suitor for Her Majesty at Kenilworth? She has invited a foreign prince to be there at the same time. I overheard her discussing the arrangements with Mr. Secretary Cecil. I expect my lord the Earl of Leicester is most put out that he must entertain one of the Queen's suitors."

I looked across to where the Earl was kneeling at the Queen's side, offering her a plate of ham. He certainly looked tired and not entirely happy.

"Oh, my lord, Earl of Leicester," Mary said in a different voice with a toss of her head. I don't know how she does it but she can do an exact imitation of the Queen. "Fie on this sun, it is too warm."

Then she reared her head back like the Earl and growled down her nose, "I am Your Majesty's to command—only stay a moment and I shall knock the sun from the sky for annoying you."

I laughed. "If the Queen ever hears you doing that, she will be furious," I said.

Mary shrugged and smiled and popped a piece of pie in her mouth.

Thank the Lord, the gentleman has stopped speaking and the Queen is thanking him *ex tempore* in Latin, which she speaks quite well. He is looking terrified. I don't think he understands what she is saying. Serve him right for going on so long.

—

Kenilworth is wonderful! Nobody can arrange entertainments and pastimes like the Earl! I know a lot of
people hate him and ask how he dare be friends with
the Queen, but undoubtedly he is a brilliant Master
of Ceremonies.

I am now sitting on the bed I am going to share
with Mary Shelton, scribbling away with my new
pen, which is very nice and smooth and not so worn
down as my old one, so I have no blots in this daybooke yet.

The chambers the Maids of Honour and the
Ladies-in-Waiting have been given are quite old-
fashioned, but on the walls the Earl has hung wonderful tapestries, all woven with silver and gold
thread that must have cost a fortune. There are
three chambers that lead to the Queen's two. The
six Ladies-in-Waiting have two of the three and all of
us Maids of Honour share the other. It has three big
beds from the Removing Wardrobe of Beds
crammed into it. We have to share beds, and Olwen
and Fran, and anybody else attending us, will have to

sleep on the floor—though there isn't very much of that, either. Still, at least we're not in tents like some of the gentlemen.

I will go back now and write of the ride to Kenilworth. I was actually feeling a little sick from eating so much at dinner. We all rode on as usual until we came within about five miles of the castle.

The Earl bowed low in the saddle and said, "By your leave, Majesty, I must ride ahead to see that all is in readiness."

The Queen gave him her hand to kiss and then he galloped away with his henchmen around him, looking, I must admit, very handsome.

We carried on slowly and the Queen called for the musicians to come up from the rear of the column. When they arrived, puffing from running in the sun with their instruments, she had them play music for us to listen to as we rode, which was very pleasant. They played Galliards and Voltas and then, when they had got their breath back, they sang some Italian madrigals for us.

We came in sight of Kenilworth and saw the castle on the hill, with its lake behind, glittering in the sun.

Then the road went through a coppice of trees which were almost ready to be cut again, so they were all leafy and full. And suddenly I noticed that the trees were hung with ribbons and little packets were tied to the twigs.

"Look, Mary!" I said, and leaned right over to grab one. Mr. Helston caught my bodice just in time to stop me falling off.

The little package was wrapped in a scrap of coloured cloth and inside was a sugared plum. I *love* sugar—it is truly the best of spices.

Mary put her knitting away quickly and grabbed as many of the sweetmeats as she could. And so did all the rest of us, except for Lady Jane, who stuck her nose in the air and looked very superior. "Really!" she sniffed. "Anyone would think you had never seen sweetmeats before."

Some new music started from one of the thicker stands of trees—very soft, high singing and harps. It hardly sounded human at all.

The column had stopped so that some of the gentlemen could grab for the sweetmeats tied to the trees, and then, just as Lady Sarah was reaching for some caraway kissing-comfits in a bag, she shrieked and giggled.

I saw why. Half a dozen men dressed as fauns, with little gold horns on their heads and naked chests and furry breeches with tails, came running from the wood. One of them had a drum and they started weaving in and out of the horses, dancing and singing that the Queen of the May and all her train were come.

The Queen firmly stopped her horse from skittering sideways and then sat and laughed and clapped in time to the drum.

The dance ended and the fauns bowed. Then the most handsome one came up to the Queen's grey horse with a big bunch of grapes and a golden cup of wine upon a silver plate, which he offered up to her.

The Queen sipped the wine and graciously ate some of the fruit. "How sweet the grapes are!" she exclaimed.

Another faun climbed a tree and made a speech that rhymed quite well, welcoming the Queen and her train to the Forest of Arcadia.

I remember when I was very little and my mother took me to entertainments, I used to think they were real. I would scream with fright at the giants and gasp at meeting the faery folk, which used to make the Queen smile. My mother kept explaining it was all in play, but it wasn't until she took me to meet the Court tumblers and the stilt-walkers and watch them putting their costumes on that I believed her. That was the first time I met my friend Masou, the tumbler.

There was the sound of hooves and a knight in silver armour galloped into view. He hauled his charger back on its haunches and then trotted up to the Queen and bowed. When he lifted his visor, we saw it was the Earl of Leicester, who must have ridden like the wind in order to change into his tilting plate.

"I am here to bring you to your summer kingdom, O most wise, most beautiful, most fair of all Queens," he boomed.

The Queen smiled, looking just as self-satisfied as Lady Sarah when she gets a poem from an admirer. "Has the Prince arrived yet?" she asked, in the sweet tones she uses when she is making trouble, which of course she was. She loves to tease her admirers—the Earl of Leicester in particular.

The Earl frowned slightly. "Of course not, Your Majesty," he said, in his normal voice again. "It would be most unsuitable for the Prince to be here before you. He is waiting three miles away until Your Majesty is ready to receive him."

The Queen nodded and, once the fauns had run

away, we rode on. As we came to Kenilworth village we saw it was all new whitewashed, with the people standing ready to cheer and wave to the Queen. All were wearing their best clothes, which I think must have been newly made of the Earl's livery cloth, for they were the one colour mostly.

Then some tumblers, dressed as dryads and faery folk, came dancing and somersaulting out and the musicians under the trees played a bright tune. And there was my friend Masou, the best boy tumbler in Mr. Will Somers's troupe, dressed as Puck in a costume of spangles and ribbons, and throwing himself through the air in flying tuck-jumps and cartwheels as he led the others.

As we passed, the faery folk threw more sweet-meats and kissing-comfits at us and we laughed and shrieked as we tried to catch them. Masou climbed a frame that was covered with flowers, and hung upside down by his legs while pelting us with sugared almonds, carefully missing the Queen. I'm sure he aimed more at me than at the other girls, and so I caught some and chucked them back, which made him grin and whisk up out of sight.

Once we were up the hill a little, we could see the big newly dug garden on our right; on the left was a big paddock where men were working to put up some very fancy pavilions painted in blue and yellow.

The Queen reined in and I recognized the mischievous look on her face. "Who can it be that is making camp upon thy sward, my lord?"

The Queen can be a terrible tease when she wants. Of course, she knew perfectly well who it was, since she had most certainly invited him. No one would dare to join the Queen upon her progress unless the Queen herself allowed it.

But the Earl of Leicester is used to being teased, and this time he smiled and answered loudly, "I know not, Your Majesty, save only that supplicants came from the far north to beg the favour of dwelling space for the while of your visit, and in my joy that you were visiting me, what could I do but agree?"

There was more coded talk, but I wasn't listening. I was craning my neck to see the camp. The men were lining up to pay their respects to the Queen. They were quite young, and very tall and handsome. A lot of them had blond hair. Lady Sarah and Carmina were whispering together, while Lady Jane did her best to look haughty, and as if she weren't staring as much as the rest of us.

Lady Helena Snakenborg came forward on her horse and inclined her head graciously. "Your Majesty, may I present my kinsmen, who come here

in the train of his grace, Prince Sven of Sweden,"
she said, indicating the line of young men. Lady
Helena has been one of my favourite Ladies-in-
Waiting, ever since she came to England in the train
of the Swedish Princess Cecilia. She got on so well
with the Queen that she was asked to stay. She has
the most beautiful pale face and fair hair and is the
calmest, gentlest person you could ever meet, and
one of the best at soothing the Queen when she is in
a rage.

"Oh!" I whispered to Mary. "They're Swedish!"

All the men were bowing. One came up to the
Queen, kneeled, and held up a package wrapped in
sarsenet. "From His Grace Prince Sven, in earnest
of his suit to you," he said with a strong accent that
sounded a bit German. He was tall, with fair hair
and a serious expression. He wasn't as splendidly
dressed as the others—in fact his sober wool doublet
suggested he must be the Prince's secretary and
translator.

The Queen beckoned Mr. Hatton to fetch the
package for her. She dearly loves to receive presents
and she opened it excitedly right there and then. As
the sarsenet rolled off, she held it up—a magnificent
hunting horn, engraved with a hunting scene and
furnished with gold and rubies.

She made a great fuss of it, passing it round to all of us, and showing it to the Earl, who had a fixed smile on his face—probably because he was jealous. Then she hung it on her belt, where it glittered in the sunlight.

We passed on up to the courtyard, which was surrounded on three sides by the castle itself. Even though it's an old-fashioned fortress from before my great-grandfather's time, it isn't at all dour or ugly. The Earl of Leicester has already installed some proper chimneys, twisting like snakes, and tall modern windows. The glass diamonds in the new windows threw back the sunset, making everything rosy and beautiful.

We waited while the Queen dismounted, helped by the Earl, who was still in armour, and went forward with her gentlemen to the Great Hall. The courtyard was full of grooms and dogs investigating. As always it seemed like mayhem, but as everyone dismounts according to precedence it was really quite organized—first the Queen and her attendants, then us, then more of the courtiers, and so on.

When it was my turn Mr. Helston steered Ginger to a mounting block, where another groom was waiting to hand me down from the pillion seat. One of my feet had gone to sleep so I had to hop a bit to join the others, who were standing in a group wondering where our quarters were to be, while more grooms led the horses past us.

A tall, fair-haired young man came along to speak to Mrs. Champernowne. "My name is John Hull," he said, bowing to her. "I am one of my lord the Earl of Leicester's henchmen and I am to show you to your chambers, ma'am." He had a very friendly smile and sparkling eyes, and I think Mrs. Champernowne liked him, for she smiled back and told him to lead the way.

We all followed, still chatting.

". . . I liked the one on the left with the dreamy blue eyes," Carmina was saying to Mary Shelton.

"His nose is too long. Mine shall be the one with curly hair and long legs," giggled Mary. "Which would you pick, Grace?" she asked.

I thought they were being a bit silly. "None," I told her. "I'm not interested in any of them." Then suddenly my foot, which was still a bit numb, slipped on a stone and twisted right over. It hurt so much I squawked and nearly fell on the steps that led up to the archway into the main keep. Somebody caught my arm and helped me to sit down on a stone wall. It was John Hull, being very courteous and sympathetic. Unlike Mrs. Champernowne.

"Tut-tut," she said with a sigh and a roll of her eyes. "Clumsy again!" She inspected my foot. "I think you have sprained it, look you. Though it isn't very swollen. We shall go up to the chamber and bandage it up. John, will you help, if you please?"

"Gladly, mistress," John said, smiling at me.

I'm sure my ankle was worse than Mrs. Champernowne said it was, because my heart was going *thud thud thud*. Everyone in the courtyard—which was full of horses and people—was too busy to notice, though.

John swept me up in his arms and carried me all the way through the arch, through the entrance hall, and up the spiral stairs to the second floor!

Even Lady Jane looked impressed by that, though I found it quite embarrassing and my face was all hot by the time he deposited me on one of the beds. He smiled and bowed out before I could even thank him.

The Removing Wardrobe of Robes had already delivered our chests of clothes, along with the Queen's. Everybody started milling around.

Lady Jane was looking for her spare smocks and throwing other people's clothes on the floor.

Sarah flounced onto a stool in front of a mirror.

"My face is utterly burned red by the sun!" she moaned. "Look! It's as if I have been haymaking. Why will the Queen not let us wear masks for our faces to protect us from the sun?"

"Stuff!" sniffed Lady Jane. "You are pink because of the Swedish gentlemen."

"I certainly am not!" snapped Lady Sarah.

"Well, I have no intention of taking a foreigner for a husband," Lady Jane said. "I had rather have a nice Englishman, like that John Hull that was so kind to little Lady Grace." And she gave me a rather nasty look, I thought. Also I am not *that* little.

I was going to say something of the sort, but Mary quietly elbowed me and whispered, "She's jealous!"

And now everyone is nearly ready. I haven't seen Ellie yet. I think she must be with the carts at the back of the train. She probably won't arrive for a while as all the gentlemen's horses have to be looked after before the grooms can attend to the carthorses. But I must go and wash my face and hands and change into white damask. Then we will all eat supper with the Queen—and so to bed early, for all of us are quite tired, even Her Majesty.

Before Dawn

I cannot sleep, what with Mary Shelton's snoring and Lady Jane's muttering. Also the Earl of Leicester has just clattered out of the courtyard with an attendance of twenty-five, to escort Prince Sven in for his first meeting with the Queen. The horses had their hooves and bridles padded so as not to wake her, but I still heard them snorting.

Last night I didn't go to bed early after all. Supper with the Queen was fun, for everyone was gossiping about the Swedish gentlemen. Lady Helena was gravely answering questions about her country. For instance, there are great dark forests whence they send us logs to build ships, and there are trolls living in the forests who will come out and eat naughty children!

When we had finished it was still quite light. The

Earl of Leicester has a hunt planned for today and he invited the Queen to inspect the horses. The Queen readily agreed. She loves to ride and she loves horses as well; I don't, so I asked to be excused because of my ankle, which was hurting a bit but not as much as I said.

I was just limping off to my chamber when I saw Ellie coming down the spiral stairs, which was lucky because I had saved her a beef pasty and some manchet bread in my petticoat pocket.

We sneaked off to the kitchen buildings, where I am not supposed to go, so she could hide behind a store shed and eat it all up. She hadn't had anything since breakfast that day. Mrs. Fadget, the Deputy Laundress, and her favourites had eaten all the dinner supplied for the laundrywomen. I've told the Queen how bad Mrs. Fadget is, but she won't interfere. Mrs. Twiste, wife of the Master Launderer, could not come on progress because she must oversee the cleansing of the laundry buildings, and the laying in of more stores of soap and ten-day-old urine at Whitehall Palace. It is a pity, because she is much nicer than Mrs. Fadget.

"I dunno what them Swedes is up to," said Ellie. "They're building a shed as well as their pavilions. What would they need a shed for?"

"Oh, that's the Prince's private stews," I told her. "Lady Helena was talking about it. They think you should bathe every single week! They'll put a brazier in the shed to heat it up, so the Prince can raise a sweat as the Turks do, and then he will take a dip in the lake."

"Load of nonsense, if you ask me," sniffed Ellie. "Everyone knows it's unhealthy to wash all the time. I think the Queen is wood-wild for bathing every month. Every week! The Prince will wash his skin away. And anyway, isn't he embarrassed about his tail?"

"Eh?" I asked.

"He's a foreigner, ain't he? So he's got a tail—stands to reason," Ellie explained.

I wasn't sure about that. "Well, I don't think the Queen would be considering marrying him if he—"

"All foreigners 'ave tails," stated Ellie firmly. "It's a well-known fact."

"But Ellie, if that's true, then Masou would have one and he hasn't," I argued.

That made Ellie pause. "Well, he's not *very* foreign, is he?"

"He's just as foreign as Prince Sven," I pointed out. "Anyway, let's go and see him."

Ellie gulped down the last of the pastry—which

you aren't even supposed to eat because it's just for holding the meat together—and we went off to find the tumblers.

They were down by the lake, having their own supper and complaining that the tents put up for them looked likely to leak. Mr. Somers, the Queen's Fool, was having an argument with the man in charge of putting the tents up. Masou was practising walking on his hands, still in his bright, ribboned Puck suit.

Ellie and I watched him for a moment. He spotted us, winked, and walked on his hands right round some trees and into a little grove, where he jumped onto his feet again.

"My lady," he said with an elaborate bow. "How wondrous—"

"Stop it, Masou," I interrupted, giving him a punch on the arm. "You know I don't like you to call me 'my lady' when we're alone."

"Masou," Ellie put in suddenly, "is it true that you don't have a tail, even though you're a foreigner?"

Masou's eyes opened wide and then he laughed. "Of course I don't," he said. "Where would I put it when I sat down?"

Ellie blushed and shrugged. "I dunno. It was just

some nonsense Mrs. Fadget was talking about," she mumbled.

Masou laughed again, and I couldn't help it—I roared with laughter, too. Ellie scowled for a moment, but then she saw the funny side and laughed as well. Masou stood on his hands again and paced up and down, still chuckling.

Somebody shouted Masou's name and, still upside down, he said, "Come and meet the newest tumbler." So we followed him as he walked on his hands back to where the other tumblers were practising.

As he came right-side up, he looked critically at the pyramid they were building. Then he turned to me. "I shall have very little time for talking with you, my lady," he said. "I have so much to do in these entertainments."

"I know, you're Puck, the Spirit of Mischief," I told him. "You nearly hit me in the eye with a sugared almond!"

"No, I didn't. I was aiming very carefully for your ears," Masou said, and grinned. "There he is—what do you think of him?"

He was pointing to the top of the pyramid, where the two dwarves, Peter and Paul, were holding up a tiny little boy with a mop of black curls. I had seen him somersaulting behind Masou at Oxey Hall.

Now he had his arms out and was balancing on Peter and Paul's hands with a look of concentration on his face.

The dwarves counted loudly, "One . . . two . . . three!" and threw him up in the air. He turned over once in midair and landed slightly unsteadily on his feet where French Louis was waiting to steady him.

"I taught him that," Masou said proudly.

The little boy came scampering over to Masou, doing a couple of cartwheels just for fun as he came. "Did you see it, Masou? Did you see what I did? Did you see? Wasn't it good?"

"It was brilliant," Masou said, clapping him on the back. "You only need to turn a little faster and you won't need French Louis at all!"

The little boy beamed with pride. He was very small and I wondered how old he was to be working in Mr. Somers's troupe already.

"This is Gypsy Pete," Masou said with a flourish. "Gypsy Pete, these are my friends, Ellie and . . . um . . . Lady Grace, who will be my patron one day."

Gypsy Pete did a somersault. "Look!" he exclaimed. "Wasn't that good?"

"Have you practised standing on your hands yet?" Masou asked. The little boy jumped up and tried to do a handstand but fell over.

Masou tutted. "Your arms need to get stronger, Pete. Go and find a tree and stand on your hands against it for practice. I'll come and help in a minute."

"Yes, Masou," the little boy said, and he ran off looking very determined.

"When did he arrive?" I asked.

"We found him doing a few tumbles with some Gypsies we saw a few days ago, and Will Somers thought he had promise," Masou explained. "He doesn't have any parents, so the Gypsies sold him to us. He's older than he looks. He's about eight or nine, he thinks, and very nimble."

Ellie had a long list of things that Mrs. Fadget wanted her to do, so we left Masou to work with Gypsy Pete, and headed back to the castle. As we did so, we saw Mr. Secretary Cecil arriving late, with all his attendants and bags of letters. He is very old and balding and boring! But he is one of the Queen's most trusted advisers. We watched as he dismounted wearily and then headed straight to his own quarters higher up in the keep.

I got back to our parlour a little later than everyone else, and found that the Maids of Honour were sitting at embroidery to keep the Queen company. The Earl of Leicester was there with the Queen as well, so I settled down to wait until she should dismiss us to go to bed.

"Now, what are your plans for tomorrow, my lord?" the Queen enquired.

The Earl rubbed his hands together, looking very pleased with himself. "On the morrow," he began, "we shall have the hunt and dinner *en plein air,* as they do in France. And in the evening, there shall be entertainment and fireworks and then—"

"When will Prince Sven be arriving?" interrupted the Queen. "I should be sure and welcome him myself, or he will think I am not interested in his suit." And she smiled at the Earl to let him know she was only teasing.

The Earl sighed. "Of course. I shall send the messenger this evening to say that you will receive him tomorrow morning. He is only three miles away and can be ready to greet Your Majesty within the hour."

"Hmph," said the Queen, taking another grape and popping it in the Earl of Leicester's mouth. "He had better not come too early as my toilette will take longer—I shall be at my best for him."

"But Your Majesty, how can there be any way of improving perfection?" asked the Earl with a look of false innocence.

The Queen smiled. They always play this kind of game when they are together, and the Queen is at her most relaxed when she is with the Earl. Mrs. Champernowne doesn't like him—and I don't, either, when he's being bad-tempered—but I think it's a pity he can't marry the Queen because of the scandal over his wife. I'm sure the Queen is only pretending to be interested in Prince Sven's suit for her hand—it's all about diplomacy and alliances being forged, as marriage always is for everybody except peasants. That's why half the courtiers talk so wistfully about being shepherds and shepherdesses who don't have to care about such things, and can wed purely for love if they choose.

So that is what happened yesterday evening, and now the sun is up and everyone is getting dressed for a new day.

And Mrs. Champernowne is scowling at me, so I must stop writing.

Later the same morning

Well, that was most interesting! I have just changed into my hunting kirtle—my black wool, because the green wool is too disgraceful to be seen, according to Mrs. Champernowne—and I am writing this while

I wait for the other Maids of Honour to do likewise. It takes some longer than others—especially Lady Sarah, who must have everything just so.

I shall begin with where I left off writing as we were dressing for to meet the Swedish Prince. We were told to wear black and white, and the Queen wore black velvet and white sleeves and forepart, so we all looked like a chequerboard when we were ready. Despite what she had said, she was up very early—and bad-tempered about it—because she didn't want to miss any hunting. The Earl had been up even earlier, of course, because he was to escort the Prince into Kenilworth.

I think it is very funny when the Queen is engaged in a courtship. Sir William Cecil fusses horribly over the arrangements. I'm afraid he is very dull— ditchwater is exciting by comparison. He never talks about anything except business and politics and administration, which is why the Queen has him as Secretary to the Council.

Anyway, as I was explaining to Mary Shelton, a courtship is like an elaborate game: the Prince or Duke, or whatever, has to pretend to be madly in love with the Queen. And the Queen has to pretend to be a shy, timid maiden! Mary thought that would be a sight to see.

This one had been carefully planned. The Queen would be casually taking the air in the garden, which has been new planted with roses to scent the air, and we would be with her. Then Prince Sven, so full of love for her that he couldn't wait for an audience, would come to find her there.

While the Chamberers finished dressing the Queen, we were all making ready in our own chamber. My ankle was still quite sore, but I was desperate to see this Swedish Prince, so I was hobbling about while Sarah and Jane sat with their backs to each other fussing about hair and smearing beeswax—pounded with little beetles from the New World—onto their lips to make them red and beautiful.

"Good morning, my lady," said a friendly voice from the door. "May I be of service?" I turned to see John Hull bowing to me. There was quite a flutter, and both Lady Jane and Lady Sarah turned to give him very gracious smiles because both thought he meant them. "Mrs. Champernowne asked me to help you," he explained. "Because of your injured ankle."

Jane and Sarah scowled at each other. As for me, I must say I think I am sickening of some distemper or other, for I suddenly felt very hot. "Um . . . my ankle is still very sore," I said, wishing it were a bit more swollen so I could show him. My voice sounded quite odd when I spoke. Definitely a distemper—I hope not plague.

I leaned on his arm to hobble down the stairs and, at the bottom, thanked him. I felt fine once we were on flat ground in the courtyard, but I did a bit more hobbling anyway as he went away.

The Queen came down with Lady Helena and we all went into the walled garden, where there are apricots trained on the south-facing walls and new roses in raised beds.

The Queen started pacing around as she always does, walking very fast, with the lapdogs skittering about behind her. Mary Shelton took the leads. As arranged, neither the Earl of Leicester nor any of the other courtiers were there, although the Gentlemen of the Guard were standing by the gates, of course, and their Captain, Mr. Hatton, wouldn't be far off.

We heard all the clattering and neighing when the Prince's entourage arrived, but of course pretended not to. And then the gate swung open and a very tall handsome man, dressed all in black velvet, with crimson lining showing in his trunk hose, came hurrying in, followed by a couple of noblemen, one carrying a long package. Prince Sven has the most amazing long legs and broad shoulders, and he has bright blond hair and quite the palest blue eyes I have ever seen.

"Vere is she, the Goddess Diana, the fairest Queen?" he demanded, in English spoken with a strong Swedish accent.

The Queen turned and put her hand to her mouth as if she were shy. Then she turned back again.

Prince Sven came striding past the rose bushes and threw himself on his knees in front of her—after one of the noblemen we met yesterday had discreetly pointed the Queen out to him.

"Your Majesty, forgive me!" he said. "I could not vait for your gracious audience. I had to come and see you in the garden, vere all the roses are ashamed to bloom if you are near." He gabbled this speech in a sort of shout, as if he were afraid he might forget the next words. I was sure he did not know what it all meant.

The Queen smiled and gave him her hand to kiss, which he did very passionately.

"Rise, Your Grace," she said. "Your presence is most welcome to us in this our realm of England."

Lady Helena was at her side, translating now, and the Prince answered in Swedish, rolling his eyes at the Queen very romantically.

It sounded funny when Lady Helena said in her sweet, gentle voice, "When my lord of Leicester came to say that you would receive me, my joy was infinite."

"Will you join us in our pleasures and revels here, then, Your Grace?" asked the Queen, and Lady Helena translated.

"Yes," said the Prince, nodding vigorously, and he beckoned over his shoulder to the nobleman carrying the long package.

Lady Helena said, "His Grace begs you will accept a small token of his love, most beauteous Diana—Artemis, maiden of the chase."

The Queen clapped her hands and laughed quite girlishly. Considering how many presents people give her, I think it's very nice how much she still likes to get them.

The man holding the package was the Prince's secretary, who had looked so serious when he delivered the hunting horn to the Queen yesterday. I noticed that he still looked rather grim-faced, as he came forward and kneeled to give this new present to the Prince, who gave it to the Queen.

She unwrapped the crimson taffety and gasped. It was a short hunting bow—the kind a lady uses, but made of ivory, not wood, and amazingly carved and decorated with gold and jewels. The Queen loves hunting and this was a beautiful bow. It came with a red leather quiver and in the quiver were the arrows. One of them was larger than the others and glittered in the sun. The Queen drew it out and we saw that the arrow was made of silver, with a gold barb and diamonds all along the fletching.

Prince Sven went to one knee again. "Vith this arrow, the arrow of your beauteous gaze, Queen Elizabeth, you have pierced my poor heart, most chaste, most puissant Queen," he gabbled, frowning with the effort of remembering.

"You gladden my heart, Your Grace," the Queen said, handing the bow to Lady Helena to hold for her. "Would you like to attend me as I make trial of your gift at a hunt my lord of Leicester has arranged for today?"

I expect the Earl had already told Prince Sven about the hunt on the way over to Kenilworth, but he bowed again and said, "Gladly." And then came lots more Swedish in the direction of Lady Helena.

"His Grace asks that he may withdraw to prepare

for the hunt," she said, and the Queen nodded graciously and let him kiss her hand again.

As soon as he was gone, we had to come up here to change. I'm not looking forward to the hunt at all. I'm really not a very good rider, despite all the lessons I've had, so I always try to trail along at the back. Last time I fell off my horse into a bramble bush, and had to spend ages pulling thorns out of my bum.

I've just had a brilliant idea for getting out of the hunting party. The Queen is in her Withdrawing Chamber, and the Chamberers are bringing in her hunting kirtle, so I'm going to see her now. . . .

Shortly afterwards

My plan didn't work. I must go hunting, after all. Hell's teeth!

Later, about three of the clock the same day

I was so pleased with my plan to get out of hunting. I got one of the Chamberers to let me bring in Her Majesty's choice of gloves, and hobbled in pathetically with them laid out on a velvet cushion.

The Queen was in a hurry, and smiled fiercely at me as if she was expecting me, though I don't know why. "Yes, Lady Grace?"

"Um . . . Your Majesty . . ." I curtsied with what I'm sure was a very realistic wobble. "May I be excused from the hunt?"

"What have you against hunting?" asked the Queen, picking up some white kid gloves with spring flowers embroidered on long cuffs.

"Well, nothing, Your Majesty," I said awkwardly. "I know it is the best way to get venison for the Court, and if deer were not hunted they would eat all the crops, but, um, I hate looking at the deer being killed."

The Queen shook her head. "You are too soft for this world, Grace, my dear. Here it is kill or be killed."

"Er, yes, but I am not at all good enough to hunt with you and my riding is still very poor . . . ," I gabbled.

"It will only amend with practice," said the Queen, drawing on the other glove and wriggling her fingers.

"And, um, my ankle is sore where I twisted it, Your Majesty."

She smiled. "Which makes no odds at all, since it

is your horse that will be running, not you. Come, Grace, I desire to have all my attendants to make a good show for the Prince. And you must overcome your timorousness with horses. I would do you no favours by listening to your fears."

I sighed. It's not that I'm afraid; it's just that I'm embarrassingly bad at it. But there was no point arguing, so I curtsied again and withdrew.

Still sighing, I went to the stairs with the others and found John waiting for me. I leaned on him and hobbled all the way down the stairs, reminding myself which ankle was the sore one as I went.

Behind me, Lady Sarah was laughing with Carmina. "At last we shall have a good run. I am so weary of ambling along roads in the sun," she was saying.

I wanted to kick her. It's not fair, she loves to ride and, what's worse, she's good at it. Her horses always do what she wants.

"Um . . . are you hunting too, John?" I asked.

"Of course," he said. "I shall follow you if it likes your ladyship."

"Oh, er, yes," I said, wondering what had happened to my tongue, which felt as if Mary Shelton had been knitting with it. Really, John Hull makes me feel quite uncomfortable and flustered, though he is most pleasant. I think it might be his eyes that unsettle me—I've never seen any so bright.

I leaned on John all the way to the Earl of Leicester's enormous stables, which turned out to be the cleanest I have ever seen, even compared to the ones at Charing Cross. The stones were gleaming and there was not a wisp of straw out of place. Our palfreys were standing waiting. I had one called Borage, with small twitchy ears, who sidestepped as I came near.

John took the bridle and brought Borage up to the mounting block. Then he helped me get myself settled into the saddle—which is always the tricky bit. The one good thing about side-saddles is that they are very hard to fall out of—though I've managed several times.

Then I had nothing to do but wait. John went off—to see about the hounds, he said—and a little while later the Queen's horse was led up to the mounting block. Then some pages arrived shouting, "The Queen! The Queen!" And everyone stood, or sat up straighter, as the Queen came into the yard.

The Earl of Leicester held the Queen's stirrup for her, as she mounted and settled herself in the saddle with her whip in her hand.

The ladies dropped back as the gentlemen rode

up to surround the Queen, each more upright and dashing than the last, all desperately trying to impress her with their horsemanship.

The Queen was now surrounded by gentlemen, with the Earl of Leicester and Mr. Hatton the closest. Sir William Cecil wasn't there—he doesn't like hunting, and was probably busy with paperwork. When everyone was ready we rode out and through the village, towards the forest.

Borage snorted and trotted to keep up with the crowd of other horses. I sighed. I much prefer lazy horses to eager ones.

The Queen was chatting to the Earl as he rode beside her, her face all lit up with excitement and pleasure. She beckoned to one of the grooms, who was carrying her quiver for her, and took out the bow to show the Earl.

He examined it gravely.

"Isn't it beautiful?' she demanded. "I have never seen a bow like it."

"It is very pretty," agreed the Earl loftily. "But will it shoot?"

"We shall try it, my lord. But do you not like it?" the Queen persisted teasingly.

"It is well enough—a fair toy for a maiden," said the Earl, scowling now. "But I fear Your Majesty shall find it bends but stiffly, and is not so apt to your hand as it may be fair to your eye."

Mary Shelton caught my eye and her eyebrows went up at this. We'd both guessed that the Earl was speaking in riddles. He was really talking about the Swedish Prince.

"String it for me," ordered the Queen.

The Earl did so immediately, pushing the bottom end against his saddle-horn without much effort, which was quite impressive. Normally you string a bow by pushing the bottom end against the ground. He passed it back to the Queen, who twanged the string a couple of times, then took an arrow, nocked, drew, and loosed. It thunked into a tree nearby. "I think it is apt for the purpose," she said, her eyes sparkling.

"Your Majesty is a true Artemis," replied the Earl, bowing from the saddle.

We had come to the edge of the forest. Waiting there was the Swedish Prince with five of his men, looking dashing and handsome in their hunting jerkins. I couldn't see John anywhere, although I had seen him going to mount.

I prefer it when the Queen waits in a hide for the beaters to drive up the game, and then shoots whatever tries to run past. But really, to Her Majesty, hunting is just an excuse to ride as fast as she can through woods and across country. She has no fear. If it would not make Sir William Cecil faint with horror, I think she would even hunt boar as the King of France does.

The Earl had organized everything in advance, so the deer had already been found by the men with lymer dogs. One of the huntsmen showed us where to go as the dogs milled around snorting and trying to find the scent. I settled myself with my whip and found John riding nearby on a strawberry roan. I was quite pleased to see him there, though I really really hoped I wouldn't end up head-first in a nettle bed.

At last the hounds gave tongue and started running. The huntsmen blew their horns, and the Queen showed off by blowing her own horn, and then grinning at Prince Sven. She used the whip, because her horse was sidestepping a little, and the gelding bunched himself straight into a canter and then a gallop.

Borage saw all this and got excited, lurching into a canter himself. And then, when I tried to pull on the reins to slow him down, he just put down his chin, took the bit with his teeth, and ignored me. Typical. I didn't want him to run fast—but there was the Queen racing ahead with the Earl of Leicester and

Prince Sven. And Borage had decided to keep up with them, instead of sticking with the Maids of Honour further back.

The Queen was leaning low in the saddle as she raced both the Earl and Prince Sven, and they went hammering through the trees and across the grass sward between them, with the Queen ahead by a neck and shouting with laughter.

Suddenly, Prince Sven's horse checked—and would likely have thrown him if he hadn't been such a good rider. He urged the animal on, but he was behind now—while I was ahead of everybody except him, the Earl of Leicester and the Queen herself! And all I could think of was hanging onto the saddle-horn and trying to move my bum in time with Borage's mad bumping as you are supposed to do. It was exciting, but also very annoying because it was Borage's idea, not mine.

I was staring ahead at the Queen, trying to do the same as her, when suddenly I saw that there was something wrong with the way the Queen was sitting. It seemed as if she wasn't as erect as she usually is. Then I realized that her saddle was slipping sideways.

I shouted sharply, "Your Majesty! Your saddle!"

The Queen looked once over her shoulder at

me—and that was when she knew her girth was broken. If she had tried to stop immediately, she would have gone straight over the horse's head, saddle and all. So she took her foot out of the stirrup and held onto the horse's mane. Her face was white, as her saddle continued to slip sideways. She looked ahead to the Earl of Leicester, but he hadn't seen what was happening.

But Prince Sven had noticed by now. He spurred his horse on and the chestnut gave a burst of speed, bringing the Prince alongside the Queen, just as the saddle went completely sideways. The Prince leaned over and caught the Queen round the waist so she could unhook her leg and then, as the saddle came off, he lifted her bodily out of it and pulled his horse to a halt.

Borage decided to stop, too, so quickly that he nearly unseated me.

I saw the Earl as he spotted the Queen's horse careering past with no rider. He turned his horse on its haunches, his face as white as milk, and hammered back to see what had happened.

He found the Queen sitting on Prince Sven's saddle-bow, pink-cheeked and breathing hard, but her eyes sparkling with excitement. "Elizabeth!" he shouted. "Thank God, for a moment I thought you had fallen. . . ." He rode close, still very pale. "Are you all right? What happened?"

I had never seen the Earl so upset. And I had certainly *never* heard anyone at all call the Queen plain "Elizabeth," as if she were an ordinary person.

"My wretched saddle fell off, my lord," said the Queen. "But His Grace the Prince caught me, as you see, and saved me."

"I am in your debt, Your Grace," said the Earl to the Prince, and even his lips were still pale. "If my sweet Queen had been hurt my life would have been a burden to me."

The Prince probably didn't understand the words but he inclined his head courteously.

"Meantime, I am without a horse and the hunt is up," said the Queen crossly. She looked across at my horse, which I would gladly have given her— except now the aggravating nag was limping as if he had strained one of his legs in his mad dash. Serve him right.

"For Heaven's sake, which of you will give me a horse?"

"Please!" Sven at once jumped down from the saddle, leaving the Queen still there. "You are welcome to take my horse," he said. "But I have no side-saddle."

You can't ride side-saddle without a proper saddle for it. But the Queen was very poor when she was young and out of favour with her father, King Henry. Because she couldn't afford side-saddles, she learned to ride astride as countrywomen do. So she simply smiled at Sven and gathered up her skirts, lifted her leg over the horse's neck and settled herself astride.

Prince Sven looked surprised at first to see that such a high-born lady knew how to ride like a peasant, but then his gaze became admiring. The Queen smiled down at him, took the reins, and kicked her heels. The chestnut sprang away, followed by the Earl.

I thought Prince Sven would wait for the grooms who were bringing up the remounts, but no, he started running at the Queen's stirrup as if he were a groom himself. I have to admit, he's got such long legs he's a very good runner. But when the Queen laughed and upped the pace, he turned back.

I caught sight of John coming up quite close by and so did Prince Sven. The Prince grabbed the horse's reins, then lifted John's foot out of the stirrup and tipped him off! Which I thought was quite rude of him, seeing that John isn't even one of his own attendants but the Earl of Leicester's henchman. Then he vaulted into the saddle and laid on with his whip. John's horse at once speeded up and Prince Sven galloped out of sight, bending low over the roan's neck.

With a lot of kicking and huffing and puffing I got Borage to limp over to the bramble bush that John had fallen into. He climbed out of it, looking rueful but resigned.

"I really don't like to gallop," I said to him, watching as Jane and Sarah raced each other past, paced by three shouting Swedish noblemen.

John had spotted the Queen's horse eating some grass just behind the brambles. He sidled up to it and caught the reins just as the horse shied away. Then he jumped up and rode bareback over to me.

"Borage looks out of sorts, doesn't he?" John said sympathetically. "I saw him run away with you and I was racing to catch up. Are you all right?"

My face went all hot. He'd been tipped off his horse by the Swedish Prince and he was asking after me?

"Um . . . I—I'm fine," I stammered. "I hope you weren't hurt by your fall?"

He laughed. "No, just a few scratches. I've fallen much more heavily than that at jousting practise."

We made the horses walk on together through the trees, with me wondering why I was so breathless. Probably all that galloping. I was quite proud I hadn't fallen off. "Do you think His Grace will catch up with the Queen?" I asked.

"I should think so," John said. "That strawberry roan is the best horse I ever rode. You did well to keep up with Her Majesty." He smiled at me.

"That wasn't me," I said ruefully. "That was Borage loving to race."

We rode around peacefully in a wide circle to go back to the castle. Then the sounds of the hounds became stronger again and we stopped to watch them hurtle past with the Queen in pursuit. We saw the stag caught in a clearing by some coppice fencing. It turned there, panting, its flanks heaving.

The hounds came boiling after it, then the Queen, the Earl of Leicester, and Prince Sven together. The Queen had her bow in her hand. Her horse stopped and she truly did look like Artemis in the tapestry on her bathing chamber wall. She dropped the reins, nocked an arrow to the string, drew, and loosed, then nocked another and loosed almost at once. You have to be a wonderful rider to shoot from the saddle. I was watching her, not the stag, because I didn't want to see it killed. I know I'm soft, but I can't help it.

The Earl and Prince Sven both cheered at once and the Queen smiled with satisfaction, so I knew the poor stag was dead.

The huntsmen had arrived, some on horseback, some running with the hounds, and they called the hounds off the kill.

The Earl and Prince Sven were both congratulating the Queen. Then the Earl of Leicester beckoned angrily and one of his grooms brought up a horse with a lady's side-saddle, but now the hunt was done, the Queen dismounted and so did everyone else.

The Master of Hounds brought the knife to the Queen so that she might make the first cut, but she waved him on to Prince Sven, who took the knife, bowed, and went over to the stag.

John helped me down from the horrible Borage. As I stepped out of his arms, he gave me a slightly odd look, but before I could ask if all was well, he led me on to the next clearing, where a repast was spread out on white cloth and musicians were playing hunting music from the trees. I was hungry and it looked delicious. There were about eight different kinds of raised pie, all beautifully decorated, and cold meats and manchet bread, and butter and cheese, with ale and mead to drink.

The Queen was already sitting on the chair that had been brought for her, and she beckoned me over to arrange her kirtle. "Well, my Lady Grace," she said, as she took one of the little pork pies the Earl of Leicester had brought for her, "what did you think of that? Did you enjoy the chase this time?"

"Well," I said, bringing her a big napkin to put on her lap, "I was very afraid when Your Majesty's saddle came loose. I never heard of that happening before. I was so scared you would fall—"

"Fie, Grace, my dear, what if I had?" she replied. "You cannot ride without falling occasionally."

I remembered how white the Earl of Leicester's face had been, but said nothing.

"Grace, I had rather you said nothing of that saddle to anyone," she told me.

"Of course, Your Majesty," I answered, feeling somewhat surprised.

The Queen must have seen my confusion, because she said, "My lord the Earl of Leicester is most distressed such a thing could have happened at his castle. I had to order him to stop apologizing to me."

"And even more distressed it was Prince Sven who rescued you," I added boldly.

The Queen gave me a warning look, but then smiled. "Quite. So we shall say nothing of it and give no fuel to gossip-mongers, since it was merely an accident, and I came to no harm."

Just then Lady Jane and Lady Sarah came into sight, so the Queen winked at me and waved me away. It looked as though Lady Sarah had gone through a hedge, for her hair was full of leaves, and Lady Jane was in a flaming temper because, it turned out, she had got lost and missed the kill.

The musicians came up and started playing again, and there was dancing, which I begged to be excused from on account of my ankle. . . . Hell's teeth! I've just realized I forgot to limp when John helped me off my horse. That must be why he looked at me oddly.

During the dancing, the court tumblers came running through the trees dressed as faery folk. They were led by Masou, as Puck, with the little boy, Gypsy Pete, running at his heels for a henchman. They danced a rustic dance which turned into a play-fight with staves, and then into a mock battle. Masou climbed into a tree and was hanging by his knees, pelting the dancers with more sweetmeats, while little Gypsy Pete sat on the branch above him and sang in a beautiful high voice.

Then the musicians played country dances, and the Ladies-in-Waiting and the older Maids of Honour stood up to dance with the Swedish gentlemen. And there was a great deal of giggling and flapping of eyelashes.

Things got rather complicated later, when the huntsmen came by with the dogs, and the dogs spotted the sweetmeats on the ground. But the massive dogfight, which immediately exploded over the delicacies, was eventually sorted out, and the Queen laughed so much that nobody minded.

We mounted again to ride back to the castle. Prince Sven rode ahead with his gentlemen, but the Earl of Leicester rode with the Queen. He was still apologizing until she tapped his head with her whip and told him to think of something nice and safe for her to do in the afternoon, since he was being such an old woman about the accident.

And so that's what we're going to do forthwith. First we are having a rest and I am writing in my daybooke. Then we will enjoy a quiet excursion to save the Earl from worrying.

Ha! That was what it was supposed to be—a gentle walk in the newly dug maze. But that's *not* how it turned out! I must quickly write this down before we go to see the fireworks.

The Earl's garden maze is too new to be very tall yet, but the hedges are there, and there are statues dotted about on pillars in the Italian manner. And the beds have been dug with different-coloured earths, to be as bright as a tapestry.

The Queen paced around the maze, arm in arm with the Earl, laughing at his jokes. He was telling her ridiculous tales of the troupe of players he patronizes, and how much they drink, and how not one of them has as much sense as a day-old chicken.

We Maids of Honour were following behind at a discreet distance—me with John, who had offered his arm to support me. This time I remembered to hobble, so he gallantly led me to a bench where I could put my feet up, and offered to fetch me something to drink. My stomach had gone all strange again for some reason, and so I agreed and just sat there alone in a little open area.

As I was waiting, the Queen walked into sight along one of the paths, and bent to sniff a damask rose that was growing near a big statue of a lion with two long tails—which is the badge of the Dudley family. Suddenly, with a tremendous crack, one of the tails fell right off the lion and plummeted towards the Queen!

Thank the Lord, the Earl of Leicester glimpsed it just in time and pushed her aside.

Being the Queen, she didn't squeal or anything, but the Earl was horrified. "Your Majesty, have you taken any hurt . . . ?"

"No, none at all," she replied. "By God, that was a strange thing to happen."

"I shall have the gardener in the stocks tomorrow, or whatever fool put it up . . . ," the Earl blustered.

The Queen was looking down at the fallen lion's tail with interest. Then she shrugged, and took the Earl of Leicester's arm again, and they walked on through the maze with the Earl apologizing all over again.

John came hurrying up to me. "Are you all right?" he asked anxiously. "I heard a crash. Were you injured?"

"No," I said. "It's quite strange—the lion's tail fell off, just as the Queen was standing under it. But mercifully, she wasn't injured, either."

John offered me his arm and I limped away for all

I was worth, until we found Mary Shelton, Lady Sarah, and Lady Jane by the exit, waiting for the Queen. John left me with them, and we waited until the Queen emerged from the maze, then went up to the parlour behind the Great Hall of the keep to have a little light supper before the evening's entertainments.

I shouldn't really be writing this, what with getting ready for the fireworks. Mrs. Champernowne keeps complaining. "Come along now, Lady Grace," she says. "Put your quill and ink away and make ready for the entertainments. You must not keep Her Majesty waiting!"

The Queen is changing her clothes for warmer ones, but I am still in my black wool kirtle with the gold brocade trim and so have a little extra time to write this, despite Mrs. Champernowne's muttering.

I can't wait to see the fireworks! I love them. The Queen likes fireworks, too, of course, which is why we have them so often. The Earl of Leicester organizes them for each Accession Day, on the seventeenth day of November, at Westminster. Everyone in London comes down the Thames in boats to enjoy them.

It's wonderful to see fireworks by the water—you get them twice, once in the water and once in the sky.

And Lady Sarah says we shall be on the lake to see these—one of the Earl's gentlemen told her. So, if I

Later this night,
nigh unto midnight

I had to stop in the midst of a sentence because miserable Mrs. Champernowne took my ink bottle away, which I think was very mean of her. She was saying I would make all the Maids of Honour late to meet the Queen—which is nonsense. But what a night it was! I can't believe so much has happened. I will write down as much as I can remember. Now, I'll start at the beginning so I don't get confused, and hope that my two candle-ends will last long enough.

Prince Sven had obviously heard about the accident with the statue, because all the way down to the lakeside he was very solicitous of the Queen. Every time she passed a statue or a pillar in the gardens, he stood between her and it, so he could ward it off her, which made her laugh.

"I have gentlemen and to spare to guard my body," she said. "But not enough well-looking princely suitors, so have a care for yourself."

Lady Helena translated this and Prince Sven bowed elaborately.

"I cannot believe you are not besieged by every eligible Prince in Europe," translated Lady Helena.

"Oh, I am," the Queen replied. "But are they well-looking?" She shook her head.

The Earl of Leicester wasn't present to be annoyed by such flirting because he was too busy with the preparations.

Sir William Cecil was fussing over news from Scotland, and the Queen was telling Prince Sven all about it—the scandal over Mary, Queen of Scots. Lady Jane and Lady Sarah think Mary is very romantic to risk losing her whole kingdom for love of the Earl of Bothwell. But her people are outraged about her murdering her husband to make way for him.

The Queen thinks Mary is an idiot—and so do I.

As we all processed down to the lake, John appeared out of nowhere, ignored Mrs. Champernowne's beady glare, and offered me his arm. I took it and made sure I limped a bit for him, but actually I've forgotten which ankle was bad now, which is a bit embarrassing. I hope *he* doesn't remember.

We talked on the way—just about things like his work as the Earl of Leicester's henchman, a post which a cousin got for him only a few months ago, and how he helped with the wonderful new

Hungarian greys my lord has bought for the Queen's stable.

At the lakeside, he bowed very gallantly to me and said, "I must leave now, I have work to do for my lord. Enjoy the fireworks."

Lady Sarah laughed and nudged me. "Perhaps I should twist my ankle soon, Grace. I believe you have a suitor."

I replied, "Fie!" I really don't know why everyone has to make so much of it—John is just helping me while my ankle's sore. Well, it isn't, but he doesn't know that. He's being kind. We are friends. What would I want with a suitor? I'm not so silly as Lady Sarah I'm-so-pretty Bartelmy.

Down on the lake there were boats ready, rowed by men in green and white—the Queen's summer colours. We went down a little jetty to board the boats. Once the Queen was settled in the biggest, with Prince Sven and Lady Helena, a drum and a pipe began playing.

There were four people in each boat, plus the rowers, and many of the courtiers were already out on the lake waiting for us. I got in a boat with Mary Shelton, Lady Sarah, and Carmina. Mary clutched nervously at the sides whenever the boat rocked.

Some musicians, still tuning their lutes, were

quickly rowed past to catch up with the Queen. Mary gasped as the wash made our boat wobble.

"It's all right," I said to her a bit mischievously. "If the boat tips us in, just think how many rescuers we'll have!"

Suddenly, the boat lurched again and Mary squealed. I leaned over to see—and there was a naiad alongside! Only it wasn't, for I recognized one of the tumblers, disguised with waterweed. He looked quite scary, and Lady Sarah squealed as well when another raised his head and splashed her. There was more splashing and ripples and out of the water rose the smaller boys of Will Somers's troupe—dressed in green fronds as mermen, and dropping the straws they had used to breathe while they were hiding underwater. Others, dressed as fauns, came running down to the lakeside, too. They formed chains and a pyramid and sang a song of farewell.

The naiads sang as well: everyone was part of the story. We were pretending to be the Army Virtuous, and we were going to storm and board the Barque Perilous, a ship of wicked giants which was near the middle of the lake. And we could see it clearly—all lit up by dozens of torches.

It was very weird, and yet believable, and if one of

the naiads hadn't started sneezing, I might have thought the lake really *was* full of water-folk!

Up ahead I saw Masou, as Puck, with his little henchmen, standing on the parapet of the barque. He gave a long speech in rhyme, which must have been very hard to learn, then invited us aboard to subdue it with our beauty.

So we all got out of our boats and walked up the boards onto the barque, which was actually a pretend ship built from stage scenery on an island in the lake.

French Louis and the strongman were there, one on top of the other, as the Giant Melancholy with a big mask and a huge hammer.

The Queen and Prince Sven came to it first. Prince Sven laughed and put his hand to his sword hilt, but Lady Helena stopped him because it's high treason to draw a blade in the presence of the Queen, unless it's in her defence.

The Queen stood and smiled up at the giant—then put out her hand, palm upwards, and said in ringing tones, "Begone, foul monster!"

And of course, the giant started to moan and cry and apologize, and we took possession of the Barque Perilous. There were some very annoyed ducks hiding in its shadows, quacking crossly every so often.

We walked along the boards to where there was seating prepared for us, and the monsters in masks being played by the Earl of Leicester's gentlemen fell back as if blinded by our light.

Then the Earl came up in his boat. He got out and led us to the benches, while Gypsy Pete clutched Masou's hand and sang a song about how he was only a minnow, but he had seen Her Majesty's beauty through the water.

The Queen listened to the song right through, and then gave the little boy her hand to kiss. He shook it solemnly, until Masou nudged him and told him what to do.

When we had all sat down, the gentlemen doused their torches and we waited in the dark, looking at the stars and wondering what would come next. I love seeing the stars when we are on progress. In London there is usually too much smoke to see the Milky Way, but here it arched over us like one of the Queen's veils.

BANG! I nearly ducked under a bench it was so loud.

A huge rocket shot off from another island we hadn't noticed, and exploded all over the sky in reds and blues and whites. We all gasped, including the Queen. With the lake around us so still and flat, it was truly as if there were two skies—one above and one below—with two sets of fireworks.

Strange music came from another platform, mainly recorders and shawms—very old-fashioned sounding—and in the darkness, while the rockets banged and crashed, it sounded as if the fireworks themselves were singing.

The Queen was oohing and ahhing and clapping her hands. The Earl of Leicester and Prince Sven sat one on each side of her. The Earl looked pleased and happy.

Suddenly, there was a loud hiss and *wheeee!* Something hot and fiery and smelling of gunpowder flew just over our heads. The Queen and the Earl and all of us ducked. The rocket buried itself in the mud by the water, where the mermen were waiting for their next song. Little Gypsy Pete was standing right by it. Then the rocket exploded and he was thrown backwards.

"Oh, my God!" said the Queen, standing up with her hand to her mouth to peer over the parapet. "That poor child."

Prince Sven tutted. He spoke in Swedish and Lady Helena translated. "How very frightening for Your Majesty. It went right over your head! Are you much alarmed?"

"Stuff!" snapped the Queen. "I am perfectly well. What about the little boy?" She turned to the Earl. "Robin, someone must run down and see what happened to him!"

The Earl of Leicester was already on his feet, white again. I realized that the Queen, in her anxiety, had forgotten herself, and called the Earl by the pet name she had for him when they were young and frightened in the Tower. He bowed quickly, vaulted the barrier, and hurried down to the shore. We could hear him giving orders. There was a flurry and gathering of torches, and then the injured little boy was carried away.

The Earl did not return, but he gave instructions for the fireworks to carry on. We stayed where we were, because it's very dangerous not to if the display is happening around you, and we all watched the rest of the show.

Prince Sven beckoned Lady Helena and started saying something quite long and serious, which Lady Helena translated. "I don't understand why everything is going wrong here at Kenilworth, most beauteous Majesty," she said for the Prince. "It is as if there is a curse. So many things! The saddle girth, the statue, the firework. My lord of Leicester should not be so careless."

"Pah!" said the Queen, looking angry. "They were accidents."

But the atmosphere was lost, and then the final fireworks—a big E covered in Catherine wheels—got stuck, and the whole frame went up in flames. It was very dramatic. And quite safe, being on another island in the middle of a lake. Though it annoyed the ducks even more.

At last it was over. We filed out to the boats again and were rowed back. The music played from the trees, but the mermen tumblers didn't return until the final part, when all the various fauns and naiads and dryads and mermen—some of them the worse for drink, too—danced and sang a song of goodnight to the Queen.

Back in the Queen's Chambers, Her Majesty stood while Lady Helena unpinned her ruff for her. I held up the mirror so she could see. She looked very thoughtful. "Lady Grace," she said to me, "how is your ankle?"

"Much better, Your Majesty," I replied.

"Then go with Mrs. Champernowne to find out how the little boy is doing," she commanded.

I curtsied and went out of the castle with Mrs.

Champernowne to the worn canvas tent in the corner of the paddock where the tumblers are staying.

Will Somers was still wearing merman face paint and talking to the Earl of Leicester. Mrs. Champernowne waited to talk to Mr. Somers, but I went round the back to find Masou. He still had one pointy Puck ear on, but he looked very upset.

"How is little Gypsy Pete?" I asked gently.

Masou sighed. "He is most grievously injured," he told me, shaking his head. "But the Earl sent his own physician to attend upon him. And he says Gypsy Pete will recover with care."

"Thank the Lord!" I gasped, relieved to hear that the little boy was not killed in the accident.

"The firework blew him backwards and he cracked his skull on a rock that was sticking up—otherwise he would have been unhurt," Masou went on. "I'd taught him how to fall and everything."

"The Queen will be glad to hear that the Earl's physician attended," I said.

Masou drew me aside. "My lord"—he nodded at the Earl, now talking to Mrs. Champernowne—"is furious. The firework master has been dismissed, for he was found blind drunk under a bush, and it was his daughter did the office of lighting the fuses.

They say she must have knocked one of the rockets off its proper placing on the frame."

Well, that explained how the rocket had gone off so near the Queen.

The Earl of Leicester came back with Mrs. Champernowne and me to report to the Queen personally. He strode ahead, not saying a word to either one of us.

Once in her chamber, we found the Queen still part-dressed and with her fur dressing gown about her. She sent the other Maids of Honour to bed, with Mrs. Champernowne herding them along, but nodded to me to stay. I sat down on a cushion near Lady Helena, who was sewing by the fire and yawning behind her hand every so often, for it was very late of a summer's evening.

I stretched my ears to listen to what the Queen and the Earl of Leicester were saying—as the Queen knew I would.

"Your Majesty," said the Earl, "I come to inform you that the young apprentice tumbler is injured but, thanks be to God, not fatally so."

The Queen put her hand to her chest and sighed with relief. "Is the poor child's family with him?" she asked.

The Earl shook his head. "He is an orphan. Mr. Somers took him in."

The Queen took out a purse and opened it. "He must have the best of care. . . ."

"I have seen to it, Your Majesty," put in the Earl. "My physician shall attend him regularly until he is fully recovered."

The Queen shook her head. "Robin, my dear, what a thing to happen. The child could have been killed." Her voice was soft and sad.

The Earl of Leicester kneeled to her and took her hand in his. "Your Majesty, I am devastated that so many happenstances should come in one day."

"Do you think there could be some kind of curse, Robin?" asked the Queen. "Some ill-will?"

The Earl shook his head. "I have no time for superstition. Not a curse, no. But be sure I shall investigate everything," he said. Then he kissed the Queen's hand and hurried away, looking harassed and tired and worried.

I almost felt sorry for him, even though he had ignored me.

The Queen beckoned Lady Helena. "I would have a posset tonight to help me to my sleep," she said. "Will you see to it? Lady Grace may unlace my stays."

That is a great honour—usually only Ladies of the

Bedchamber help the Queen undress. Lady Helena lifted her brows, because generally I would be the one sent chasing after a posset for Her Majesty. But maybe she thought the Queen was being kind because of my ankle.

The Queen called me to her as Lady Helena backed out. "Well, my Lady Grace," she said. "My Lady Pursuivant. What do you think? What were the tumblers saying of the accident?" She knew I would have spoken to Masou. That was why she sent me, after all.

"Well, they found the firework master blind drunk under a bush, and he has been dismissed," I told her.

She nodded. "So I should hope." She looked down and frowned and shook her head. "I don't understand it. My dear Robin is so careful usually. He has such an eye for detail—he organizes everything. But so *many* accidents."

"Three in one day," I agreed. "It is odd. The saddle, the lion's tail, and now the firework."

"I am afraid people will gossip. They will say that my Lord Leicester is careless of my safety, or that he is cursed. I would silence the gossip-mongers, Grace. My lord the Earl would never endanger me."

I smiled and curtsied. "Do you want me to investigate, Your Majesty?"

"Yes, my dear Lady Pursuivant. Though no wild adventures, please. It may be that some enemy of the Earl of Leicester's desires to discredit him, and has thus conspired to sabotage the entertainments. Before we have any more tragedies, find out what lies behind these events."

I went on my knees to her and kissed her hand, though what I really wanted to do was hug her, she sounded so sad and anxious. I am proud that the Queen has trusted me with something so important.

"Of course, it will be hard for you to find things out for me if you must attend me all the time," the Queen went on. "We shall give out that your ankle, which I see is much better, is a great deal worse. And you must remember to continue to hobble whenever people can see you. Then you will be less busy. Whatever you may find, you shall report solely to me. Now, I'll raise my arms so, and you shall undo my bodice lacings first."

I had all the lacings of the Queen's kirtle and bodice undone, and the sleeves off, by the time Lady Helena arrived with a creamy brandy posset for Her Majesty.

"Go to bed now, Grace," she said to me, and so I curtsied and backed out, then hurried up the stairs to the Maids, our chamber, where I found everyone readying themselves for bed.

Ellie was picking up smocks and holding a napkin for when Penelope Knollys should finish cleaning her face. Olwen was unlacing Lady Jane, and Mary Shelton was helping Carmina out of her gown. And so I sat down on the bed to write this, until all the flurrying should die down.

I always enjoy listening to the daft things the other Maids of Honour say.

Lady Sarah was talking about me when I came in. "I don't know . . . ," she said, frowning at a particularly spectacular pimple on her chin and not noticing that I had arrived. "You can see what Grace likes in John—he's attentive and he's a wonderful rider—"

"Prince Sven is a wonderful rider, too," Carmina broke in. "And much taller."

"The Prince smiled at me when I passed him a plate of Maids-of-Honour, and he didn't even know that they are little cheese tarts. So I told him," Penelope remarked.

"I like that tall nobleman that is his lieutenant, the one with blue eyes and the green doublet," said Carmina dreamily.

"I like his secretary," Penelope responded. "The tall one who always looks so mysterious."

"You mean grim and disapproving," sniffed Lady Sarah. "I'd say his lips are too thin, and you know what that means. Thin lips speak an ungenerous heart—all the face-reading books say so."

Then the conversation turned to the Queen—and I soon realized she had been right about the gossip.

"Of course, the Queen could marry Prince Sven," Lady Jane said to Lady Sarah. "Even Parliament wouldn't mind, since he's a proper Protestant, even if he is only a Lutheran. Everyone would approve—and then she could have a son of her body."

We aren't really supposed to talk about the Queen's private life, but of course everybody does. All the time. Penelope and Carmina giggled—well, it is difficult to think of a lady as old as the Queen having a baby.

"The Earl of Leicester would be devastated," Lady Sarah said in a tragic tone of voice. "The Queen is his first and only love."

"Apart from his wife, whom he probably murdered," Lady Jane said nastily. Everybody else shushed her and looked round nervously. "If he could do that, he could do anything. I believe he's behind all these so-called accidents," she added.

"Then you know nothing of the matter." Lady Sarah sniffed. "The Earl of Leicester loves the Queen ardently and would never do anything to hurt her."

"Of course he wouldn't." I agreed with Lady Sarah, which doesn't often happen. It gave Sarah something of a shock, because until then she had not even realized I was in the room!

"But it's very odd that there have been three accidents in one day," said Carmina thoughtfully. "First, Her Majesty's saddle falls off at the hunt—"

"How did you know?" I asked.

She tossed her head. "Everybody knows," she said. "They all saw the Queen riding to the dinner *en plein air* astride Prince Sven's horse—the place has been abuzz with it. And the groom in charge of the Queen's saddle has lost his place, too. Then there was that statue that broke in the maze—and you know, statues do not usually break, do they?"

The other girls were hanging on her words.

"And now a firework nearly takes the Queen's head off!" Carmina shook her head. "You mark my words, I think this is a curse!"

"Whose curse?" breathed Sarah, very interested.

"Well," whispered Carmina, "it's probably somebody in the Robsart family wanting vengeance for

79

poor Amy. What about that cousin who won't stop trying to get the Earl arrested for it? Maybe he paid a witch to put a curse of ill-luck—"

"Nonsense!" interrupted Penelope Knollys unexpectedly. "It's the Scots. There are probably Scottish spies skulking around here and trying to kill the Queen for capturing *their* Queen."

"The Queen thinks it's just . . . accidents," Mary Shelton said uncertainly, and everyone shouted her down.

Ellie has just brought me a fresh smock, and winked and rolled her eyes at the nonsense they're talking. And I am not going to listen to any more silly gossiping. Time for bed.

About midday—in the maze

As I am acting as Her Majesty's Lady Pursuivant, I must make a record of my findings, I think. So, no matter what Mrs. Champernowne says, I have decided to carry my daybooke and penner in my embroidery bag wherever I go. And here I am, sitting upon a stone bench hidden in the maze, and this is my record of my investigation—although I am very tired, thanks to Mary Shelton and her snoring. She kicked me twice when once I did doze off, saying I was talking again—which I am sure I was not.

This morning Her Majesty had on a wondrous satin gown all painted with creatures—birds and butterflies mostly. Carmina clapped her hands at how lovely it was, which pleased the Queen. After we had all filed into her chamber, she smiled and told us to gather round.

81

"Now, I have a splendid jest for to play upon my Lord Earl and His Highness the Prince, and indeed upon all the gentlemen," Her Majesty began. "They fawn upon me, but how well do they know me?"

She paced about a little. "The day after tomorrow, our last day here, there is to be a masked ball, and at it I shall be the Queen of the May. You shall all be dryads and naiads and I wish you to study with the Dancing Master for to make a pretty dance of it—the tailors of the Removing Wardrobe of Robes will help with your costumes.

"Now," she went on, with a significant look at me, "as my Lady Grace has hurt her ankle, she shall make a speech in rhyme instead of dancing with the rest of you."

Lady Sarah and Carmina sighed with relief, which I think is unfair—I'm not *that* bad at dancing.

"However"—the Queen stopped for effect and her eyes sparkled—"I shall be incognito at the ball— Lady Sarah shall play the part of me as the Queen of the May . . ."

Lady Sarah clapped her hands to her mouth and went bright red—for it's a great honour to play the Queen. She dropped a curtsy.

". . . and I shall be but one of your company," the

Queen went on. "We shall see if any of the silly men that profess so much love for me will notice the change at all."

We all clapped our hands at this and laughed, and then everyone was talking at once.

The Queen held up her hand for silence and caught my eye. I'm sure she thought up the masque to stop the Maids gossiping—as well as every attendant, henchman, and servant in the place.

"I shall be joining some classes with the Dancing Master, so shall find out also if what he says is true, that you are *les vaches*, that you thunder like tournament chargers and that you insist on talking constantly throughout."

There was an embarrassed titter from everybody, except Lady Sarah, who was looking very worried.

"What is it, my dear?" the Queen asked her.

"Oh, Your Majesty," gasped Lady Sarah, "I don't know if I can . . . if I can be as *regal* as you."

The Queen smiled at this for, quite by accident, Lady Sarah had said the exact right thing. She may have more chest than the Queen, but when the Queen walks into a room, everyone else in it becomes instantly uninteresting and unimportant.

"I can give you lessons on how to be queenly,"

Lady Jane said, looking very superior. And then she caught the Queen's glare and faltered. "Unless Her Majesty can spare the time . . ."

"*I* shall give Lady Sarah instruction," the Queen said firmly.

I quietly slipped out while they were all babbling and arguing over whose complexions would be best as dryads—tree spirits, who wear green and brown—and whose would be prettiest as naiads—water spirits, wearing blue. The Queen saw me go and nodded.

Nosy Mrs. Champernowne said, "Ah, Lady Grace, where do you think—?"

"It is well," the Queen broke in. "There will be dancing practice shortly and Lady Grace is excused. She is to walk about as much as she can to help her ankle."

Mrs. Champernowne sniffed and looked suspicious, but she couldn't do anything. Ha ha!

I found Ellie in the kitchen garden with a huge basket of washing, hanging shirts and smocks on hedges to dry in the sun. She didn't pause when she saw me but kept on wringing out sleeves and spreading the clothes on the hedges. She looked cross and I wasn't sure why. "Ellie?" I said. "Did you hear what happened yesterday?"

"Masou's too busy to talk to me, being as he's Puck," she said, squeezing a falling-band collar viciously. "Is it true what I heard, that my lord the Earl fired a cannon at the Queen for her dallying with the Swedish Prince, and missed her, but hit Gypsy Pete?"

"Not quite," I said. "It was really a firework and it went the wrong way by accident."

"What's your young man John think of it, then?" she asked, throttling another shirt.

"I don't know, I haven't seen him today," I said, and then gaped. "*My young man?* What are you talking about? He's just been helping me because my ankle was sore."

"Well, I saw you going calf-eyed over him," said Ellie with a wink.

"You couldn't have!" I told her.

But she just shook her head and looked disbelieving, as she wrung out some hose. "I hate that Mrs. Fadget," she said. "She says I did the ruffs the wrong colour, so I had no dinner yesterday because I was redipping them."

Since Ellie never has enough to eat at the best of times, this was serious. I looked around to see if anyone was watching and then I carefully helped her put the rest of the laundry out. Getting her some food was quite urgent, so we went round to the kitchens, but everyone was too busy cooking for the entertainment tonight.

Some of the Earl's men were working on the Banqueting House in the garden—it's the second-best one, brought from storage at Court. The canvas was once all painted with saints, but they got painted out and replaced with classical goddesses and gods—which are a bit blurry. The men were decorating it with fresh leafy boughs so it would look more like a bower.

Ellie and I went and looked at it. "Some of the food for this afternoon might be in there already," I said. "Come on, let's have a look."

The entrance was shut and there was a lad standing guard. As we watched, John came out looking very busy and serious, and then another person went in carrying a tray of fruit jellies gleaming with sugar. There were wormwood leaves hanging by the door to keep the flies away.

All the leaves and branches gave me an idea. If we gathered some plants and flowers, we could pretend we had come to help with the decorations, and then the lad at the entrance might let us in. So we went into a corner of the orchard and picked some ferns.

Then, with Ellie carrying them behind me, I marched up to the boy outside the Banqueting House and said, "My lord asked me to help arrange tables for the banquet."

He bowed and opened the flap for us. So in we went, with Ellie half-hidden under all the leaves.

We went over to the main table, where there was a wonderful marchpane and sugar plate subtlety in the likeness of a bear, standing on its hind legs, holding a ragged staff. The bear was coloured brown-black with liquorice and had white sugar plate teeth and a red marchpane tongue. Although I think he was meant to look fierce, he looked quite a gentle, sweet bear really.

Ellie didn't need any telling. She dumped the ferns on the floor and started lifting the napkins laid out over the plates, swiping a square of marmelada sweetmeat here, a stuffed date there, and eating them hungrily. She put a few in her petticoat pocket for later. Meanwhile, I wrapped ferns decoratively around the plates to hide the crumbs.

Ellie looked longingly at the bear. "I love liquorice," she said.

Well, only the Queen is supposed to eat the subtlety. But usually she doesn't eat very much because the sugar makes her teeth hurt. So I scraped a finger along the modelled bear fur, but it was quite solid. The bit at the top where the bear's head was didn't look as if it had quite dried yet, so I dragged a bench over and stood on it, with Ellie steadying me from behind. The marzipan fur round the bear's ear looked softer, so I reached up to break a little bit off, when—

Suddenly, Ellie gasped and let go. I lurched and my elbow knocked the top off the ragged staff and broke the bear's ear. A big lump fell to the ground, making the bear look as if he had been in a bear-baiting ring. I glimpsed Ellie lifting the tablecloth and rolling under the table, still stuffing dates into her mouth, which is when I realized someone was coming in.

I was a bit stuck and it would be daft to jump down and run. So I took a deep breath, grabbed some of the leaves out of my belt, and carefully wrapped them round the bear's head where they would hide the damage.

"My Lady Grace," John said. "I'm glad to see your ankle is better."

"Er . . ." Oh, Hell's teeth, not John, I thought. I wobbled, looked down, and realized that the piece of bear's ear and the staff were on the floor right next to the bench. Oh, no. What if he noticed? I wobbled again and he put up an arm to steady me. A thought struck me. If he was looking up at me, he wouldn't be looking down at the bit of bear on the floor.

"Er, yes, a little," I replied. "I have been excused dancing practice and Mrs. Champernowne said I should help, so I am just putting a victor's wreath on the bear here. Isn't he handsome? Such a fierce-looking bear. And I don't know who could have done the sugar-work. It's amazing, isn't it—especially as the Earl isn't married, is he . . . ?"

I chattered away about how exciting it all was, and what was planned for the afternoon, and the dancing and so on, and I thought I sounded exactly like Lady Sarah at her very worst. In fact, I'm embarrassed to write it down. I was feeling more and more silly, so I thought I'd better come down from the bench, only I tripped on the edge of my kirtle and lurched against the table before John could stop me.

I nearly knocked it over, subtlety and all, because the tables were only trestles and boards covered with a tablecloth. I caught a glimpse of Ellie making furious faces at me while she held it all together from underneath. John grabbed the bear and steadied both it and me.

"Oops," I said, and cringed at how foolish it sounded. "I am beyond belief clumsy this day. I had best come down, I think." And with John holding my hand for me, I stepped down and shook out my petticoats, while Ellie's long skinny arm came out from under the tablecloth and grabbed the lump of bear's ear and the top of the ragged staff, and whisked them out of sight.

"Have you any part to play this afternoon?" I asked, walking away from those dangerous tables and trying not to laugh. "I know not what the entertainment—"

"There will be jousting," John replied. "We're putting up the Tilting Yard barriers now."

I clapped my hands. "Wonderful!" I said. "I love to watch it. Will you be tilting?"

John laughed. He does have a very nice friendly laugh. "No, my birth might be well enough, since I am a gentleman, but I have not the wealth for it, or the skill, either."

We were just going to the door when I spotted that Ellie was having trouble getting out under the stretched canvas. You could hardly see her, for the table was in the way, but I glimpsed her bum and a hand as she tried to find a loose place.

"Um . . . who will be jousting?" I asked, pausing

and putting my hand on John's doublet to stop him, because I was afraid that if we came out, he might see Ellie just as she escaped. "My Lord Earl, of course, but who else?"

"He has sent for all the tilting plate and the chargers to come up from London, so whoever of the Queen's gentlemen that likes him to try," John replied. "And Prince Sven may do so also." He was holding the tent flap open for me now, so I went out graciously and stood between him and where I thought Ellie might emerge.

"Who do you think will win?" I asked him.

"Well, my Lord Earl is one of the finest jousters in England. But Prince Sven has quite a reputation as a jouster himself." He offered me his arm again.

I thought he was delightfully courteous, though of course he is not a suitor—far from it! So I took his arm and did a little bit of hobbling, and steered him away from where Ellie was squeezing out under the canvas. I saw her out of the corner of my eye, puffing and red in the face, with her cheeks bulging like a squirrel's.

I limped away from the Banqueting House with John in tow. He was talking happily about the betting on the various gentlemen in the jousting, which saved me from having to think of any more foolish things to say. I don't know how Lady Sarah does it, I really don't. Then I noticed that his right hand was bandaged and stopped still. "Whatever happened to your hand?" I asked.

"It is nothing," John said, dismissing it. "I scorched it on a poker when I was mulling some ale for his lordship. I have put comfrey ointment on it and it will soon be better."

He said nothing more, while I wracked my brains for something else to talk about. What *do* you talk about with youths? They are such strange creatures.

We had just come round by the orchard again, when Ellie came running up, dropped a very respectful curtsy, and said, "Please, ma'am, the Queen wants you," and winked at me.

"Oh, of course," I said, laughing with relief. "I expect it's to look at the costumes for the masque, and I so hope I am a dryad, for I think green and brown will become me well—don't you think so, John?"

He smiled. "Perfectly, my lady," he said, and then bowed and went off towards the castle.

Ellie went with me round to the stable yard, where we collapsed, laughing, in the corner.

"Fie!" said Ellie at last, wiping her face with her

apron. "That was a bit close. Do you think he saw anything?"

"No, I hope he was too dazed with my prattling," I said, suddenly feeling gloomy and hot in the face. Whatever would John think of me now? "Did you at least get something to eat?" I asked Ellie.

"Oh, yes," Ellie replied, and licked her lips. "I ate so many marchpane dates I feel quite sick. I haven't got any room for that bit of subtlety you so kindly broke off for me. Do you want it?"

"No," I said, and shuddered—I hate liquorice root. "You have it."

"Suit yourself. Are you going to do any pursuiving now, my lady?" Ellie enquired.

"Of course . . . ," I replied.

"Only Masou's in such a taking about little Gypsy Pete getting hurt, I want to find out who's been causing these accidents and get 'im," Ellie went on darkly.

I felt a little guilty. I hadn't actually done any investigating yet—though I had been excused dancing classes. The Queen would be disappointed if she knew. Why can I not think in a straight line when John Hull is about? Perchance I have a tertian fever?

—

There weren't many people about the stables, since many of the horses were out being exercised by the grooms. There was one middle-aged man in his shirtsleeves and jerkin, standing on top of the manure heap, tidying it up and combing it flat—which is usually a job done by one of the youngest boys, for obvious reasons.

I squinted up at him and realized it was Sam Ledbury, who is one of the Queen's grooms. He has helped me on and off horses, me protesting all the while, ever since I was little. And he has looked after the Queen's horses for ever. Of course, he is the Earl of Leicester's man—but the Earl is the Queen's Master of Horse, after all.

"Hello, Sam!" I called. "Why are you up there?"

He had a very miserable expression on his face but he smiled and propped up his rake, then jumped down from the heap. "Now then, my Lady Grace," he said, pulling his cap off, "what brings you here?"

"Er . . . Her Majesty asked me to look at her saddle from yesterday," I said, all in a gabble because, of course, she hadn't exactly asked that, but you could count general investigating as asking.

Sam looked miserable again. "I just don't understand it," he said, heading away from the manure heap towards the main tack room. "I don't understand it at all. I checked that saddle myself with one of the Gentlemen of the Guard, not half an hour before the horse was tacked up, and all of it was perfectly sound. Yet it came away and nearly took the Queen with it. I don't know," Sam mused, shaking his head gloomily, "maybe I'm getting too old for this game. That a saddle I put on a horse should have threatened the Queen's sacred life . . ."

I patted his arm. "I'm sure the Queen doesn't think it was your fault."

"Hmph," said Sam. "The Master of her Horse does. 'E told me not to come to work until he's satisfied what 'appened, and when I said I couldn't keep away from the stables, me—what else would I do?—'e said I could work on the manure heap. So I thought I'd tidy up where the young scalawags have left things messy."

Messy? I never saw a tidier, better organized stable!

We were at the door to the ladies' tack room. Sam took a key from a lace round his neck and opened it. The place was full of side-saddles on long poles from one end to the other, and bridles hanging up beside them. At the other end, on the workbench, was the Queen's gold-embossed, red leather saddle, with tools all around it.

I went over, trailed by Ellie and Sam, and looked at the saddle. I could see where the two important straps had come loose—the girth and the crupper strap that goes around the horse's haunches. I examined them closely.

They hadn't broken or torn. I blinked and peered closer. "Look," I said. "Ellie, can you see?"

She looked where I pointed with my finger and gasped. "Oh, yes," she said. "Cuts."

"What?" said Sam, with his nose practically touching the saddle. "I can't see nothing."

"I think you need good eyes to see them—or perhaps one of those miracle lenses for people with bad eyes," I said. "There are little cuts between the stitch holes—here, and along here—as if someone used a very sharp knife to cut through the stitching."

"You mean . . . ," Sam said slowly.

"Yes, someone purposely cut the stitches so that when the Queen rode fast—which she always does when she gets excited on the hunt—the straps would give way."

"Saints above!" exclaimed Sam. "So it was done a-purpose. My God. Who would do such a thing? A scurvy Scot? A Frog? We must tell my lord—"

"No," I interrupted. "I think it would be better to keep quiet about it until we know more."

Sam started to look stubborn, so I added, "We don't want anyone to say it was you, Sam."

Sam gulped and stepped back. "But I never would!" he said frantically.

"No, of course you wouldn't, Sam," I said. "I just want to be sure of the facts before I talk to Her Majesty. Can you move the saddle and hide it? Just for a short time? It could be evidence."

He thought for a moment, then nodded and took the saddle off the workbench. He hid it behind the bolts of leather in the corner, moved the other saddles along, and brought one of the Queen's spare saddles to go on the workbench instead. "It needs work anyway," he said. "And the saddlemaker don't know which is which."

"You checked the saddle before you tacked up the Queen's horse?" I asked him.

"Aye, and it was in perfect condition, no stitches loose nor anything. I put it on, done up the girth, and checked it. Then one of the young gentlemen came and led the horse out for the Queen to mount."

"Do you know who it was?" I enquired.

"Well, I don't," he confessed. "I think he was one of the Earl's men, or perhaps one of Secretary Cecil's—not anyone from the stables anyway. Didn't recognize 'im, but then I often don't when we're on progress."

"Hm . . ." I looked at Ellie significantly. "If you should see him around the place, could you tell me, Sam?"

"Of course," Sam replied. "You don't think he could have . . . Why, surely he wouldn't have had time?"

"Even so, I'd like to talk to him," I said.

We left the ladies' tack room and he locked it carefully behind us. He shook his head again. "I can't believe someone would want to hurt our sweet Queen," he said. "Is it true a statue nearly fell on her yesterday, as well? And there was a magic thunderbolt that a black magician loosed off which hit one of the tumblers."

"No," I said. "That was a firework. Thank you very much, Sam. We must be going now."

I could hear dancing music coming from the Long Gallery inside the castle, and the thunder of elephants—well, Maids of Honour. I was so glad I didn't have to parade up and down, and pirouette, and try to remember which move came after which, and bump into people, and fall over and get wailed at by the Dancing Master. I can do dances I know well, but not new ones. I don't know how anybody remembers them quickly, and as for twitter-pates like Lady Sarah, who pick them up in the twinkling of an eye—well, it's just annoying.

But I was glad Sam had reminded me about the statue, because now we had found that one of the accidents was no accident at all, I was very suspicious indeed about that statue and intended to investigate further.

Ellie came with me. When I asked anxiously if she'd get into trouble with Mrs. Fadget, she snorted. "I'm not having you wandering about the castle without an attendant," she said firmly. "It ain't right. So I'll attend you and worry about Mrs. Fadget after—the old cow!" she added, which showed she wasn't quite as unworried as she said.

So Ellie and I went and looked at the statue of the lion with two tails. I don't know why that's the Dudley family badge, though it might be something to do with the fact that a lion has his power in his tail—so if he's got two, he's twice as powerful.

When I looked at the place where the tail had been, it didn't look as if it had cracked naturally. I could see some white marks, as if the stone had been hit very hard with something metal. And behind the statue there was a flattened place in the bushes, where someone had clearly been standing.

"Hm," said Ellie, poking the white places with her finger. "It looks like it was chipped."

"It *was* chipped," I said. "And recently."

So I sat down at once right here in the maze, to write it all down so I wouldn't forget anything. And I think it's very interesting that— Oh, somebody's shouting for me.

Later this day:
afternoon—at the tilt

I must catch up with all that has happened, so I am writing this secretly at the joust.

It was Mary Shelton shouting for me in the garden, so I went over to her. She was very red in the face from dancing practice. "You are so lucky to get out of the dancing," she moaned to me. "I don't think it's fair—why should we have to go over and over it and get shouted at? Anyway, the Queen wants you because you have a speech to give, and one of the Earl's house-poets has written it."

My heart sank. It would probably be very long, and the rhymes idiotic. It's a terrible pity nothing much rhymes with *Elizabeth*, because very often poets call the Queen *Eliza* so they can rhyme it with *surprise her*, or worse.

We all headed back into the castle. Ellie came with us so she could gather some dirty laundry and use it as her excuse for being away so long.

When I got to the Long Gallery, all the Maids of Honour were there, as well as four Ladies-in-Waiting—so there were ten naiads and dryads in all. They were fanning themselves and drinking mild ale thirstily. It looked as if it would be a very vigorous dance, but that's how the Queen likes them.

The Dancing Master, Monsieur Danton, was drinking aqua vitae by the gulp. "Now zen, milady Grace," he said, "You 'ave just a few steps, *vous comprenez?* Only a very few. And zen you say zis speech . . ." He gave me a long scroll and I looked at it with foreboding. It began, "All hail, fair England's fairest Queen. All hail, our gracious Eliza . . . ," which told me all I needed to know.

The Queen arrived, pages running ahead of her shouting, "The Queen!" She had been doing governing, closeted with Sir William Cecil and a pile of papers to do with Scotland. She looked in a very bad temper, and practically shoved Cecil through the door, to be rid of him before he could start prosing on about some other administrative problem. Then she came and stood by the Dancing Master, who bowed and cringed. She smiled at him, and spoke to him in French, and then laughed at his protestations. I really wanted to talk to the Queen privately and tell her what I had found out, but I didn't get the chance immediately.

"Come!" said the Queen, clapping her hands. "Let us see this dance."

The other five Maids of Honour lined up, curtsied, and began to skip and hop, first to one side, then the other. Then they made a ring, circled each other as in a Bergomask, and then formed a Farandole Snail Shell. At the end of it, I read my speech as best I could, stumbling over all the odd words.

Next, the Queen took Lady Sarah's place—which made everybody tense up—and did what she could remember of the dance. Monsieur Danton kept stopping the musicians, playing wearily in the corner, to correct her steps, and after some changes had been made to show off her jumping abilities, the dance was really quite good.

Then the Queen gave Lady Sarah some Queening tuition—as in holding up your head, walking confidently, moving slowly, and always expecting people to make way for you. Lady Sarah was surprisingly good at it, all things considered, which made Lady Jane look very shrewish indeed. I'm sure she thinks *she* should be the one pretending to be the Queen, even though she looks nothing like Her Majesty. But it is hardly Sarah's fault that the Queen chose her, so there's no call for Jane to sneer like she does.

At last the Queen said she was satisfied, and we filed down the stairs to the Hall to eat our dinner. I was quite hungry, as I hadn't eaten any of the sweetmeats in the Banqueting House. But, alas, it was one of those dreadful formal meals where you sit about for ages while the food is paraded around and carved very slowly and then brought on big platters.

The Queen sat under her Cloth of Estate and received local gentlemen, and the Earl of Leicester's friends—not that he has many. Nobody likes him much at all—the courtiers are all jealous of his friendship with the Queen.

We were scattered about the tables in order to talk to the gentlemen, and I got a very dull man who talked about sheep the whole time.

After the second cover, when we were about to remove to the Banqueting House, the Queen beckoned me over. "Well, Lady Pursuivant," she said, "what have you discovered?"

"That two of the three accidents were no accidents, Your Majesty," I whispered.

She drew in a sharp breath and frowned. "Are you sure?" she snapped. "Who caused them?"

"I don't know that yet, Your Majesty. I know only that your saddle fell off because someone had cut the stitching, and that the tail fell off the lion because someone had chipped at it—mayhap with a chisel."

"Good God! Is someone trying to kill me?" she demanded. She was speaking to me out of the side of her mouth as she smiled graciously at a local knight who was proposing a toast to her.

Her Majesty was pale but I could tell she was furiously angry.

I thought about it very carefully. "Possibly, Your Majesty," I said seriously. "If I may be excused this afternoon also, perchance I could find out more of the firework. I could slip away while everyone is watching the jousting."

Her Majesty nodded.

I hesitated. "And may I have Ellie from the laundry to attend me?" I asked.

"Of course," the Queen said. "That is very sensible of you. It's always best to have a witness to these things." She sent a page for paper and pen and then wrote a note for me, saying that I had need of Ellie and that Ellie had her permission to assist me.

As we were talking, Masou and the fauns came tumbling in, and invited us to a bower to eat the fruits of the earth.

We all stood up and processed, with music, to the Banqueting House. There were the delicious sweet-meats that Ellie had raided, but we all exclaimed with excitement because there were also heaps of soft fruit and clotted creams and custards for us to eat.

I fetched a big bowl of strawberries and raspberries and cream, after the Queen had been served with them. I don't know how the Earl of Leicester managed to find so many strawberries. He must have gardens full of strawberry plants somewhere, and I hoped I could find some for Ellie, as I didn't dare put any in my pocket lest they be squashed and stain my petticoat.

Lady Sarah and Lady Jane were greedily eating raspberries, while Mary Shelton had at least two custards.

When the time came to go out to the jousting in the Tilting Yard, I slipped away to the lake, where I had seen the women washing shirts on some rocks. Ellie was standing there scowling, with her arms folded, while Mrs. Fadget shouted at her.

"Oh, we're very high and mighty, ain't we, Ellie? Ay must attend 'Er Grace. Ay can't do the washing what ay'm paid for. Oh, no, Mistress Ellie, she's too high and mighty for that."

What I really wanted to do was hit Mrs. Fadget, but instead I went up behind her and coughed. She turned, about to shout at me, too, but then saw who I was and dropped a very begrudging curtsy. "Yes, ma'am, how can I 'elp you?"

Well, there's nothing angry adults hate more than smiling politeness, so I took a deep breath, smiled, and said, "I'm afraid I must borrow Ellie again to attend me on an errand for the Queen."

Mrs. Fadget went purple.

"Here is the Queen's note for you," I went on, very politely, and gave her the piece of paper upside down. Of course, as she couldn't read she didn't know that, though she recognized the Queen's signature from its elaborate curly shape.

She grunted and jerked her head at Ellie, who came trotting over and curtsied to me.

Then we hurried away, leaving the other women to

grumble at both Mrs. Fadget and Ellie herself, which hardly seemed fair.

"I knew Mrs. Fadget would be horrible to you," I said. "I don't know why the Queen doesn't sack her."

"Because she's a very good starch-woman," said Ellie. "Anyway, she was right to shout at me this time, because I didn't go back when I said I would. I went down to the village."

"Why?" I asked curiously.

"To try and find the firework master for you," Ellie explained.

"And did you?"

"Not exactly. I found his daughter, though." Ellie led me out through the gate and down the lane to the village, which still smelled of whitewash.

The peasants' children were playing some complicated game with a ball made of rags. I watched them for a moment, wondering what it must be like to have so many other people to play with. I was often lonely when I was little, as there are few children at Court. Most ladies go home to their estates to have babies and then leave them there with wet nurses, and return to Court without them. My mother was very unusual in having me with her in Court. But then, her friendship with the Queen was special, too.

Ellie led me round the back to a barn and a leather tent. I could see a cart inside the barn, and a girl sitting spinning with a drop spindle beside the tent, but no sign of any firework master.

The girl was clearly expecting us, for she stood up when she saw me, wound up the wool, and curtsied. She looked very tense and unhappy.

Ellie went straight up and confronted her, hands on hips. "Now then," she said. "Is your father awake yet?"

Silently, the girl went into the tent and came out again, shaking her head.

"Is he ill?" I asked, worrying about plague again, for in summer there is always that possibility.

"In a manner of speaking," sniffed Ellie. "Seeing as 'e's drunk."

"Is it true your father was drunk last night as well?" I asked.

The girl nodded, looking close to tears. "But I told the Earl it's not like him to be drunk and incapable," she said. "I've told 'im and told 'im but he didn't listen. He just said 'e'd never use us for fireworks again, and we was to be gone. I don't know what's to become of us."

"You shouldn't have been so careless and hurt Gypsy Pete," declared Ellie fiercely.

I glared at Ellie, then turned to the girl and said gently, "I want you to tell me everything that happened last night. I may be able to help you."

She invited me to sit down on the tree-stump she had been using, and after some concentrated glaring from Ellie, she fetched me some mild ale. Then she told me that she was called Rosa Herron, and her father was Master John Herron, freeman of the Guild of Firework-makers and Ordnancers.

They had travelled up from London to Kenilworth with an escort from the Earl of Leicester, in case anyone tried to rob them of the fireworks on the way. Then, when they had arrived, they had set up the firework frames with the help of some of the Earl's men.

"But they was all checked carefully," explained Rosa. "When you do a firework display they're all mounted on wooden frames so they go in the right direction, and my lord the Earl was very careful of it all. He checked the frames himself in the daylight, and he and my father did the calculations to be sure they would be safe. My father can read and write and use Arabic numbers, too," she added proudly.

Then she put her face in her hands. "But he'll be driven from the Guild for sure, for his fireworks were not safe and my lord the Earl will never use us again and . . . and . . . that poor little boy . . . ," she sobbed.

I went over to her and patted her back. "You know, Rosa," I said softly, "there were two other accidents that happened around the Queen yesterday. They turned out not to be accidents at all. Perchance the same is true of the firework. . . ."

Rosa calmed down enough to talk, and I went back and sat on the tree-stump. I took a sip of the mild ale she had given me and nearly spat it straight out again. It was horrible—vinegar fly must have got in it, for it was as sour as old guts.

Rosa saw my expression and looked downcast. "I'm sorry, my lady, it's been in the heat too much. You could have some of the double ale that one of Mr. Secretary Cecil's men brought yesterday?"

I was surprised. One of William Cecil's men? Usually it would be the lord of the castle who would supply the meat and drink to his workers.

Well, I was quite thirsty, and I do like double ale— though the Queen doesn't, so we don't have it much. So I nodded, and Rosa went and brought out a large earthenware jar of double ale and poured some into a pewter mug for me.

"Everything was set for the evening," Rosa went on, "and we went out on the firework island to watch the revels. We saw you and the Queen go out to the island, and then when it was time to set off the fireworks, I found that my father had fallen asleep and I couldn't wake him at all—"

"Drunk!" Ellie said disapprovingly, and Rosa flushed, so I nudged Ellie to be quiet. It's no good upsetting people when you want to hear the full story.

"You know," I said, "many men drink too much sometimes. My uncle, Dr. Cavendish, occasionally staggers and it's difficult to make out what he's saying."

Rosa smiled back at me a little. "Father does drink a bit too much, that's true," she said carefully. "I wouldn't deny it. He's always liked his ale and he drinks from his own flask of aqua vitae, too—but he's *never* so distempered of drink that he cannot deal with the fireworks. Never."

"But yesterday he was," Ellie pressed.

Rosa sighed and nodded unhappily. "He was so deep asleep, even hitting him didn't waken him."

I took a sip of the double ale, which was quite strong and had a slightly musty taste—not unpleasant—probably from being brewed with herbs.

"Well, it was time for the fireworks," Rosa went on. "I thought I'd best set them off myself, and I was just going with my fire pot to the first of the frames with the rockets on, when . . ." She flushed and looked down.

"What?" I asked, taking another sip.

"You won't believe me," she said.

"We'll see," I persisted.

"Well . . ." Rosa took a deep breath. "A merman, all covered with weed, rose up out of the water. He snatched my fire pot and hissed at me to keep away, and I was so frightened I ran away back to my father."

The sun was hot on my head—I was annoyed with myself that I had not remembered to bring a hat with a brim, or a veil to keep my complexion pale. I blinked hard and took another sip. "What did the merman look like?" I asked, hiding a yawn.

"He was bedecked with weed, and his face was very frightening, all covered with scales like a fish and long hair like waterweed."

There was something wrong with my eyes but I couldn't think what it was. The sun had made me very thick-headed and I started to feel woozy. It was rather embarrassing. Double ale doesn't normally affect me so quickly. "And what did he do when the fireworks had finished?" I asked with an effort.

Rosa shook her head. "I didn't see him go. I just heard a splash."

"Hm," I said, swaying slightly. I thought Ellie looked funny, the way her face was changing shape and getting bigger and smaller. The world went round me as if I were dancing, and I slid down onto the ground. It was really too much effort to get up, never mind the problem of staying awake, so I shut my eyes and fell fast asleep.

—

I woke to find water being splashed on my face and half my bodice laces undone. Rosa was wringing her hands and Ellie was squatting next to me, patting my cheeks.

"You fainted," she said. "I never seen you do that before. Are you ill?"

And suddenly a thought struck me: I had only started feeling sleepy when I drank the double ale! I sat up quickly, which made my head rock quite a lot, and I pushed Ellie away. "That ale," I said. "Where is it?"

Ellie looked at me as if I was going bedlam, as she

puts it, and pointed at the mug I had put down just before I fell over—I had only had about three sips from it.

"Put the jar of double ale in the tent and hide it under something," I ordered. "I'll wager there's laudanum in it to send someone stupid and sleepy."

"What?" asked Rosa. "But it came from Mr. Secretary Cecil. One of his men, dressed in his livery, delivered it."

"You might've fainted," objected Ellie to me.

"Well, let's test it then," I said. "What animal might like to drink ale?"

"Pigs," said Ellie. "They get the brewer's swillings, so they're used to ale."

So all three of us went down to the Earl's swineherd's cottage, where there was a sow with her piglets in a small sty. I found a water bowl and poured a little of the double ale into it, and Ellie hopped over the gate quickly and put it down on the ground.

Two little piglets came over and slurped it up— they were handsome red Tamworths, very lively and curious—and then they looked at each other in a puzzled way, lay down on their sides, and went to sleep. Their six brothers and sisters were busy rooting in their food trough and stayed awake.

"See?" I said. "The piglets that drank the double ale have gone straight to sleep, but the others are all wide awake."

Rosa whistled. "Father had a couple of pints of double ale this morning when he woke up and realized what had happened. That must be why he's sleeping now. *And* why he passed out last night . . ."

"We need to find the liveryman of Cecil's who brought the drink," I told Ellie. "Perchance it was he who dressed as one of the mermen last night, to come across to the island where the fireworks were and frighten Rosa."

"In which case, he was the poor jesting soul what fired off the firework that went so near the Queen and injured Gypsy Pete," added Ellie.

Rosa blinked at her in puzzlement. "Why are you sorry for him?"

"I feel sorry for him because of what I'll do to 'im when I catch 'im, that's all," Ellie told her darkly.

I was thinking hard, though my head was still a bit fuzzy from the laudanum. "No, Ellie, I don't think it's just some liveryman of Cecil's playing practical jokes. This is too serious. He wouldn't have done it without orders from Mr. Secretary."

Everyone knows that Sir William Cecil is the Queen's wisest adviser and the best administrator in the country. But it is also well known that he and the Earl of Leicester hate each other violently. They have to work together because the Queen insists and because they both serve on the Privy Council, but you can see both of them bristling when they are near each other. So that could explain why the accidents were happening—mayhap Cecil was trying to get the Earl into trouble with the Queen.

"It means," I continued urgently, looking at Rosa, "that you must keep that ale safe and hidden as I said, and *don't* let your father drink it. It's important evidence."

"But we haven't got anything else for him to drink," said Rosa. "The Earl wouldn't even pay us our expenses from London after what happened last night."

I fished in my petticoat, found my purse, and gave her some shillings for to buy ale. "If I send for you to come, or if the Queen asks you about what you've told me, then you can explain what happened. Otherwise say nothing to anyone, especially not to Sir William Cecil's men, do you understand?"

Rosa nodded and stood looking at the shillings in her hand. "I promise," she whispered.

Ellie had warmed towards her. She patted Rosa's

back. "You watch," she said. "My lady will sort it all out for you, see if she don't."

Rosa smiled back at her, and I felt quite nervous to think that she was relying on me.

Ellie and I went back up to the castle, where we could hear the *thuddity-thud* of horses' hooves and the ringing crash of lances breaking. We slipped in at the side of the benches where everyone was watching the jousting. It had only just started—there must have been an amazing amount of speechifying between the Earl of Leicester, as the Champion of May, and his friend Henry Carey, the Queen's cousin, as the Black Knight of Melancholy, before the jousting proper began.

Ellie went down to the standing areas behind the barriers to watch with the other servants, and I came here to sit with the other Maids of Honour.

Mary very kindly brought my embroidery bag out for me—she finds jousting boring and is still knitting away at the baby's jacket. But I've been sitting scribbling in my daybooke to record all my discoveries before I forget anything. As soon as the Queen withdraws, I will go to her and explain that perhaps Sir William Cecil is connected to all the accidents which have occurred.

I have bolted down supper as quick as I could to write this—now we are sitting in the Hall to watch a play by Terence in Latin. The Queen is laughing at the jokes and so are some of the courtiers, but I don't know enough Latin to understand.

It was a wonderful afternoon's joust. The Swedish Prince did very well—he not only beat the Black Knight of Melancholy; he beat the Earl himself as well, by two lances broken to the Earl's one. And so he got the prize, which was a very rich horse's harness and caparison. The Earl was furious and Henry Carey wasn't too pleased, either. Now the English gentlemen are sulking and the Swedish gentlemen are crowing.

After the joust, the Queen withdrew to her chamber to rest and deal with more papers of State. I followed her, and Ellie came along as well. The guard at her door waved me away when I tried to go in, and so I said loudly, "But the Queen bade me speak only to her in this matter."

I heard Her Majesty's voice then. "Let her enter," she ordered.

I left Ellie at the door and went in. I found the

Queen sitting with her feet up on a footstool, and her stays unlaced, poring over a legal document.

After I'd curtsied, I told her exactly what Rosa had said and what I'd found out about the double ale, and who had brought it.

The Queen frowned when she heard it was one of Sir William Cecil's men. "Are you sure?" she asked. "Where is the firework master's daughter?"

"I can send for her at once, if Your Majesty pleases," I said, thinking I could ask Ellie to fetch her.

"Please do," the Queen replied. "And then wait in the anteroom until I send for you both."

As I left to find Ellie, the Queen called the gentleman who was guarding her door and ordered him to fetch Sir William. Then she waited, tapping her fingers on the arm of her chair, her face cold and angry.

I went into the little anteroom where servants wait, and found Ellie there petting the Queen's dogs.

"Please go and fetch Rosa for me," I said. "The Queen has just sent for Sir William Cecil."

Looking very serious and excited, Ellie nodded and then ran out the door.

I waited and waited, putting my ear to the door of the Queen's chamber every so often. Mrs.

Champernowne says eavesdroppers hear no good of themselves—but sometimes you just *have* to know what's happening.

At last I heard Sir William Cecil's voice. "I am very glad you sent for me, Your Majesty, as I have just had another dispatch—"

"That can wait, Mr. Secretary," the Queen interrupted frostily. "I would first desire to hear what you know of the accidents of yesterday."

"Terrible carelessness," said Cecil. "I understand the groom that neglected your saddle when preparing for the hunt has been demoted by my Lord of Leicester, and—"

"Someone had cut the stitching with a sharp knife," the Queen interrupted again.

"Good heavens!" Cecil exclaimed.

"And the statue, Cecil," the Queen went on, "had been tampered with. And as for the firework that went off course—someone brought the firework master drugged ale to drink. While he was asleep, the miscreant came in the guise of a merman, and lit the fuses so that one of the rockets nearly hit me and did in fact injure one of the tumblers. And so he was well-nigh a murderer—in that he was reckless of the consequences of his actions—as well as a traitor."

"I am horrified . . . ," Cecil gasped.

"Cecil, do you know who sent that ale?" the Queen demanded abruptly.

"No, Your Majesty," Cecil replied.

"I find that strange, since it came from you and was brought by one of your liverymen." The Queen's tone was as sharp as a sword blade. It was terrifying.

"What? I never sent ale to a firework master! Wh-why should I do so? I—I am n-not—" Cecil was stammering.

"Silence!" roared the Queen. "I do not believe you have been directly endangering me. But it is possible you have been engineering accidents to discredit my dear Robin, the Earl of Leicester."

I was fascinated. I peered through the crack in the door and saw Cecil as white as a sheet. "I would never—" he began.

"Have you been trying to make me doubt the Earl, and believe he is becoming careless of my safety, so that I would turn my eyes to the Swedish Prince and like him the better for saving me? It would make sense, would it not, Cecil?"

There was silence. Then I heard the thud of Cecil's knees on the floor.

"Your Majesty"—his voice sounded choked, genuinely devastated—"I would never . . . I have never—"

"The ale for the firework master was delivered by a lad who wore your livery," rapped out the Queen.

"But it was not sent by me or *from* me," said Cecil, his voice strengthening. "I utterly deny this accusation, Your Majesty. I know not who has been speaking against me—"

"Not against you, no, for she barely knows the significance of what she tells me," said the Queen.

"*She?* Hmph. Some foolish hysteria no doubt—"

"Enough!" the Queen snapped.

Ellie panted into the antechamber with Rosa behind her—her face washed and her white cap tied on tightly. She looked terrified, as well she might.

I knocked on the door and called softly, "She's here, Your Majesty."

"Call all your attendants together and we shall see which one of them brought the ale," said the Queen to Cecil.

Sir William bowed and withdrew.

I brought Rosa in and she kneeled to the Queen.

"Now, my dear"—the Queen spoke softly and gently—"be not afraid, only show me honestly, when they are gathered, which was the man that brought the double ale."

A few minutes later, all Cecil's secretaries and clerks and serving men were lined up in the orchard.

At a gesture from the Queen, who was standing in the shade of an apple tree, Rosa went along the row of men, frowning at each face. She was shaking so hard she could hardly walk, so I went with her, holding her hand.

The tension mounted. Sir William, watching from beside the Queen, looked nervous and unhappy.

Rosa walked from one lad to the next, looking searchingly at each face. At the end of the row she stopped and shook her head. "Not one of them is the lad that brought the ale," she said.

Cecil didn't look very relieved. "One is missing," he said. "Which is it? Ah, yes, fetch Alan Yerd."

Two of the others sped off to get him. They didn't come back for ages—and when they did, they brought a tall man, wrapped in his cloak, with only his shirt and hose under it.

"Is that the man?" demanded Sir William.

"No, sir," said Rosa.

"Why did you not come when you were ordered to?" demanded Cecil.

The man looked very embarrassed. "Somebody stole my livery doublet and jerkin, and I've no other that's fit," he said nervously.

"*What?*" shouted both the Queen and Cecil together.

"Yesterday morning, before I got dressed, I went to the Wardrobe men—for I had asked them to brush out my doublet for me. Only they said they had already given it back to my friend who came for it. But I never sent no one to get it and so—"

The Queen was laughing with relief. "My dear Sir Spirit," she said, using her nickname for Cecil, "I am so glad that I was mistaken," and she held out her hand to Sir William for him to kiss.

"Indeed, Your Majesty, so am I," Cecil replied.

And I felt glad also. For though Sir William Cecil is, assuredly, the most boring man in England, I have always believed him honest and would have been sad to find him otherwise.

"Now we must find out who stole the livery," the Queen said decisively.

Rosa was dismissed, and a short time later the Wardrobe's Chief Tailor and his skinny apprentice were standing in front of the Queen.

"Well, Your Majesty," said the tailor, "it was Martin here what let the suit of livery be stolen, though he's a good lad and able as any of us with a needle—"

"Quite so," agreed the Queen. "Now, Martin, be not afraid—tell me what happened."

Martin stood on one leg and scraped the other

one up and down the rush mat. "I'd brushed it out, see, Majesty—the livery I mean, Mr. Yerd's livery from Sir William Cecil, see. And then the gentleman what came and got it was tall like Mr. Yerd and had his hat pulled down, and he gave me a penny for the good job I'd done, and I thought it was Mr. Yerd, see—"

"Did you see his face?" asked Cecil.

"N-no, sir," stammered Martin. "My eyes aren't too good, that's why I was 'prenticed at the Wardrobe."

So that was a dead end.

I will continue my investigations as soon as I can escape from this tedious play. At least I have removed a suspect. I am now convinced that Sir William Cecil had nothing to do with the accidents, though somebody went to considerable lengths to implicate him—stealing his livery to wear.

In spite of the gossip, like the Queen, I simply do not believe that the Earl of Leicester himself can be behind the accidents. They reflect so badly upon him, since he is responsible for all the arrangements, and besides, I believe he truly loves Her Majesty and would not do anything to put her at risk. Perhaps the Earl is cursed, but I doubt it. . . .

So, who is left? That is, who remains that would

wish to discredit the Earl of Leicester and, perhaps, Secretary Cecil as well? There is the Swedish Prince, of course. He would certainly be pleased to see the Earl of Leicester discredited, and would not be displeased if the dislike between the Earl and Sir William were to worsen. But how could he have done it? All his attendants are Swedish. None of them speak much English—and the tailor's apprentice didn't mention that the man who came for the livery had an accent. He would certainly have noticed if the man had been foreign.

It is very perplexing. I must devise a way of finding out more about the Swedish nobles and the Swedish Prince.

Thank the lord, the play is ending. I see that Lady Sarah has a new admirer. She has been batting her eyelashes at him through all the play, and now he has found an excuse to speak with her. Lady Jane is looking put out. She does hate it when Sarah gets more attention than she.

Later this day—midnight

Lady Sarah's flirting gave me a marvellous idea for a plan to investigate the Swedish Prince—though I am not sure if it will work.

After the play we went back to our chamber, but then Lady Sarah decided to go and find some moon-lit cobwebs to put on her spots. I spent some time devising my plan and then realized I needed to talk to Sarah, so I went to look for her.

I found her just as she was coming in, accompanied by Olwen, carrying the cobwebs on a twig.

I walked beside her as I wasn't at all sure how to ask what I wanted to ask, so I began a long way away, ready to work up to the main point. "You're very good at getting along with gentlemen and talking to them and so on," I said.

Lady Sarah looked at me rather suspiciously. "Hm," she said noncommittally.

"Well, it's just that I never know what to talk about," I told her, which is true in a way. "So what do *you* say when they talk to you?"

"My goodness," said Sarah, a little smugly. "Why are you suddenly interested in gentlemen, Grace? This is new."

"Well, um . . . I just wondered . . . ," I mumbled, nearly overcome with sheer embarrassment.

Sarah smoothed her satin gown. "It wouldn't have anything to do with dear John Hull, would it?" she enquired.

"Oh, no, of course not. Not at all," I said, and

wondered why my face was feeling so hot—I wasn't anywhere near a brazier.

Sarah smirked, as if she didn't believe me. How annoying.

"Just . . . er . . . gentlemen," I pressed on. "You know, like the . . . er . . . like the Swedish gentlemen."

She laughed and patted my arm. "Don't fret, Grace," she said. "It's pleasing to see that you're turning into a proper Maid of Honour at last. After all, we are all here to find a rich nobleman to marry and adore us, aren't we?"

"Um . . . ," I said, speechless for once.

"But I don't think John is really suitable," Sarah continued. "He doesn't seem to have any family or lineage. But you can practise on him."

"No . . . truly, I just want to talk to the Swedish gentlemen, really . . . ," I persisted.

"Of course," Sarah said. And then she actually winked at me! "Now, let's see. There's no point in pulling your bodice lower—no breasts. Or letting your hair escape a little—too straggly."

I scowled at her.

"Hm. The idea, you see, is to let the young gentlemen think it's their idea to talk to you," she explained.

"And isn't it?" I asked, surprised.

"No, of course not. Lord above, if you left it to the men, there would be no dalliance at all! So you must be as visible and as beautiful as you can be—and then you . . ." She did something peculiar with her eyelids, sort of looking down and then up and smiling. "Like that," she said.

"Like what?" I asked, still not sure.

She sighed. "You look up at them through your eyelashes. And then you look away. And then you look back just for a second and look away again."

"Oh," I said, more confused than ever.

"And then when they come to you, pretend not to be at all interested in them," she went on.

"Won't they get discouraged?" I asked.

"No, being ignored is good for young men," explained Sarah. "They are so vain, they think they must be noticed by everyone. So if they find one girl who ignores them, they must get her attention at once."

"I see," I said, though I didn't.

"So, when they have run through the usual nonsense"—Sarah was waving her hands—"'What is a beautiful flower like you doing in the Court dunghill? . . . Do you like the music? . . . Have you lately come to Court? . . . Are you the Queen herself? . . . Oh, surely you must be . . .'"—that sort of thing—then you ask them what they have just been doing, or what they are just about to do. And they'll say something like they just played a game of tennis with so and so and beat him, or they're about to play a veney at sword practise and are bound to beat so and so, or they're thinking of buying a horse and are planning to look at him . . ."

"Oh," I responded, feeling rather bewildered.

"And then you have to look admiring and interested, and let them tell you all about it. And then find an excuse to get away when you can't bear it any more." She patted my shoulder. "Then they will think you are not only beautiful, but mysterious and charming as well!"

It was sounding more and more complicated by the minute. I thought about Masou—I never have to do anything like that with him, he's my friend. Why be so complicated?

"Oh, and you must laugh at *all* their jokes—no matter how bad," Sarah added. She laughed—sort of a cross between a trill and a gurgle. I have observed before that it seems to remove most men's wits completely. I don't think I will ever get the way of it.

"Will you come with me tomorrow morning, Sarah?" I begged.

"You don't need me to attract John, he's already chasing you," said Sarah, with a toss of her hair.

"No, I meant to see the Swedish gentlemen."

"Oh, the *Swedish* gentlemen," said Sarah, with a waggle of her eyebrows that I thought was quite unnecessary. "Hm. Well, they are very nice to look upon—and at least we won't have to listen to a blow-by-blow tale of the latest notable tennis match."

"Won't we?" I asked.

"Well, we will, but they will be speaking Swedish or Latin so it doesn't matter. All right. Tomorrow morning, before the men of the Removing Wardrobe arrive with our costumes, I will go with you to the Swedish encampment and we will discourse a while with His Grace, Prince Sven's, attendants. Perhaps we shall even be honoured by a meeting with Prince Sven himself. And it will be perfect practise for your sweet John, whom you were staring at this evening." And she winked at me again!

I bit back the urge to tell her I was not interested in John and didn't care if I never saw him again, and just tried hard not to get any redder in the face. It is true, however, that when I finished writing in my daybooke, I thought I might as well watch the mumming. And it just so happened that John was there with the rest of the Earl of Leicester's henchmen. Quite an accident, in fact. I hadn't realized he would be. I thought it was very clever of him to understand the Latin jokes, and I spent a short time watching how he pushed his fair hair back. And then the play was suddenly over, and we clapped, and us Maids of Honour went with the Queen for our supper.

Honestly, I really don't know what Sarah is on about over John.

THE FOURTH DAY OF AUGUST,
IN THE YEAR OF OUR LORD 1569

Afternoon

I am in the Maids of Honour, our chamber, writing this instead of learning that horrible great long speech I have to make tonight, but I had rather do anything than that. At least our disguises for the ball have come from the Wardrobe, and there is a great to-do as everyone scrabbles to unpack them.

Early this morn, after we had broken our fast, the Queen sent us all out to take the air and get out from under her feet, since Sir William Cecil had more news from Scotland and she must deal with it.

Sarah gave me a very significant look so I went along with her, away from the rest, who had decided to play cat's cradle in the shade of a big tree by the lake. Some of the gentlemen were fishing in the lake, which may have had something to do with it.

Sarah and I walked away from the lake and round

the Hall towards the paddock, with Mary Shelton puffing after us. "Where are you going?" she asked. "Can I come?"

I didn't really want her to, especially after Sarah said, "Grace wants flirting lessons."

"Oooh!" said Mary, looking at me curiously. "I see. Well, can I have some, too?"

"Of course," said Sarah very graciously.

I caught Mary's arm and whispered, "I've got a good reason for wanting to talk to the Swedish gentlemen—just go along with it and help me."

"Oh, not Jo—"

"No, of course not," I interrupted. "It's nothing to do with John!" I was quite annoyed about it. Why does everyone keep harping on about him? Anyway, I've hardly seen him at all lately.

"All right, Grace," said Mary equably. "Don't pinch my arm."

Sarah had us line up in front of her and then turn sideways. "Look down, then up through your lashes. That's right, Grace. Down and then up. That's better, Mary." She sounded like Monsieur Danton.

"Oh, very good," she praised Mary. "You fluttered your eyelashes, too."

"No I didn't," said Mary. "I got a bit of dust in my eye."

Sarah sighed. "Now, look at me and then look away."

We did.

She sighed again. "You could giggle a bit, too," she suggested.

Mary snortled like a pig. I did my best, but what was funny?

"Not like a donkey, Grace—he's supposed to find it attractive," Sarah said wearily.

I tried for silver bells, like Sarah.

She hurried over, looking anxious. "Are you well, Grace? Perhaps you have a sore throat?" She wasn't being sarcastic: she doesn't know how. She was sincerely worried. That made me laugh properly, and she sighed again. "Well, I suppose that will do. Now, supposing he says, 'Where are you going?' What do you say?" she demanded.

"I don't know," I said. Mary just looked puzzled.

"You say, 'Where are *you* going, sir?' You never answer a question, you simply ask another question. And sooner or later he'll start to boast and then you can relax."

Something suddenly occurred to me. "But that's what the Queen does with ambassadors!"

"Exactly," Sarah agreed. "Now, I forgot to tell you one very important thing. If he's droning on and on about some horse's wonderful fetlocks, and you're going to die of boredom, you simply fan yourself a little more, breathe in and out quickly and then . . ." She sort of melted to the ground, where she lay very gracefully with her feet together. Mary and I rushed over and she looked up and grinned. ". . . you swoon. He'll get very excited and rush for help, and you can always recover quickly if he gets funny ideas about loosening your stay laces!"

"Why would he do that?" I asked, and both Sarah and Mary rolled their eyes at me.

"So, practise. Fan, breathe hard, one leg goes, the other follows, sit and flop. Lovely," said Sarah enthusiastically when we did it. "Put your hand to your head first and say, 'Oh . . . I feel suddenly dizzy . . .' so he knows you have fainted, because he is only a man, remember. You shouldn't do it too often—only if you're too bored for words or if you need to escape from an embarrassing situation."

Mary and I practised a couple more swoons because it was quite fun to see how daintily we could fall and lie there with our feet together. And then we got up and marched on to the paddock.

"I don't know," said Sarah, eyeing me dubiously. "In truth, I think I would need at least a month to teach you anything much. And we'll be leaving John behind in a day or so."

I really think that was uncalled for. I really do. Why should I care about leaving John behind? And anyway, he could come along with us, couldn't he? With the Earl of Leicester? It's possible.

I tried some more looking down and then up, and nearly sprained my eyeballs.

The Swedish gentlemen had stretched a net between two trees near their tents and were playing a very vigorous game of battledore and shuttlecock, with much leaping and swiping and arguing (in Swedish, of course). I wanted to wave to them, but Sarah said we must just stand there and watch.

Soon the game became even more wild, with the shuttlecock losing feathers and one of the rackets losing a string. One of the gentlemen took his doublet off to play in his shirtsleeves.

"Ah," said Sarah wisely, "they've noticed us. Do what I do."

And they had. They abandoned their game and came over and started talking in a mixture of Swedish and Latin.

Sarah giggled when one of them bowed and shouted, "Beautiful! Beautiful!" in a very strong accent, so I tried to do a girlish giggle, too. I have to admit it did come out sounding a bit like a donkey.

"*Latinamne linguam intellegis?*" said one of them.

Mary shook her head. "I know what that one means," she whispered. "He wants to know if we speak Latin."

"No," shouted Sarah. "English!"

They were trying to say something, shouting in Swedish, and then one of them said something about *quae sunt nomina vestra?* and Mary thought that meant something to do with names. So Sarah pointed to herself and said, "Sarah," and Mary did the same, shouting, "Mary," and I was going to do it, but they were all gathered round Sarah saying things like, "Sarah beautiful," and suchlike, which was really quite annoying.

"Is there anyone who speaks English?" I asked, to lots of blank looks. I elbowed Mary. "Go on, say it in Latin."

She looked alarmed. "I don't know much Latin. Um, er . . . *adestne aliquis qui Anglice loqui potest?*"

That got a long sentence with the name Eric in it, and then one of them turned and pointed. Eric was the grim-faced clerk, in a sober suit of black. He came over and looked very disapproving at us, which wasn't surprising because Sarah was still giggling. "Can I help you, ladies?" he asked. He didn't sound very friendly and he had a very strong accent. "Vat do you vant?"

"Are you the only one who speaks English?" I asked.

He scowled at me. "Vy do you vant to know?"

"I just wondered." I thought of asking about the accidents. Maybe I could sort of allude to them. "Everyone is very impressed with the Prince, and the way he saved our Queen from falling off when her saddle slipped."

"Yes," said Eric, frowning a little bit less. "His Grace vas vorried—he says there seem to be many dangerous things happening here."

"What are you gentlemen planning to do for the masked ball?" asked Sarah, doing the looking-down-and-then-up thing. It didn't work on Eric, though.

"His Grace and all of us vill be there. Ve look forward to it," said Eric stiffly, not sounding as if he did at all.

"*There* you are!" came Mrs. Champernowne's voice as she puffed towards us from the castle. "Will you come within at once? The gentlemen of the Removing Wardrobe are here, look you, and you must try on your disguises. Come along with you."

So that was the end of that, though the Swedish gentlemen waved cheerfully to Sarah as we went back to the castle.

—

I've written it down, though, to be honest, I think it was a waste of time. All we found out was that the Swedish gentlemen don't speak English—and the only one who does, the Prince's secretary and translator, Eric, speaks with an accent. Not one of them could have disguised himself as Sir William Cecil's liveryman, or a merman for that matter, without his accent being noticed. Which means it couldn't have been one of the Swedish gentlemen who collected the livery from the Wardrobe, or delivered the double ale to Rosa and her father, or scared Rosa away at the fireworks. So I am no closer to working out who could be causing the accidents at all.

At the moment, the last remaining bit of floor is covered with chests full of disguises for the masque. All the other girls are grabbing them and trying them on. They go over our normal black or white Court gowns and are made of silks and voiles, in green and brown for dryads, and blue and white for naiads.

Mary Shelton is trying on a naiad costume, which looks quite becoming on her. Sarah is standing in a corner, being fitted by one of the Wardrobe tailors for her Queen of the May costume. It is being made in costly cloth of silver and white velvet because, of course, she will be disguised as Her Majesty the Queen. My mask is very pretty, with its green ribbons and silken leaves, but Sarah's is quite wonderful. It has elegant white feathers and diamond spangles around the eyes. She has just put it on and she looks very mysterious as it covers all of her face, not just her eyes. She is looking in the glass, turning this way and that to see the diamond sparks glitter, while the tailor is trying to let her bodice out at the sides with panels of white velvet in the side seams. I wonder how many of the gentlemen will fall for the Queen's trick—and I wonder how the Queen will look dressed as a dryad!

"Oh, Sarah," said Carmina, who was swishing her blue naiad ribbons about, "you will look beautiful. Are you nervous?"

Sarah nodded. "I wish I were just being a dryad now," she said. "I have to make a speech, too. Will you help me learn it, Carmina?"

Which reminds me, I suppose I really should start learning *my* speech—Mary has said she will help me. I hope I don't tangle my tongue on all the *Eliza*s.

Later, upon the eventide

We have had a light supper and I have to practise some dancing now, as well as that speech. . . .

The Queen just came in. She looks happier. She has been for a walk in the gardens with the dogs and that always relaxes her. It isn't relaxing for anybody else, mind. She walks incredibly fast and is impatient if you can't keep up. Now she is putting on the dryad costume over Sarah's white damask gown. Oops! Lady Helena had to put two handkerchiefs down the front for padding! But with the green and brown leafy mask and her hair dressed simply, she really does look like Sarah.

—

Hell's teeth! I am wearied to death. We just went through the whole dance three times, with Her Majesty taking Sarah's place and Sarah processing in stately fashion as the Queen.

My feet are aching and I have to learn that speech again, for I forgot it when the Queen was scowling at me. I don't think she likes being called Eliza much, either.

—

Well, that was very exciting, although I fear I am in disgrace again. Here I am sitting on the bed, scribbling, as the other Maids of Honour come clattering up the stairs. I must speak to the Queen as soon as she has finished being undressed.

As soon as we had finished rehearsing, we had our hair dressed and then we gathered in readiness to go downstairs, the Queen among us. Sarah looked wonderful with all her red hair dressed with diamonds, and when she paraded along with her head up, she did look quite a lot like the Queen. She waited in the Queen's Withdrawing Chamber while the Queen came with the rest of us, trailing green satin leaves.

We processed into the Hall, which was full of all the courtiers and Swedish gentlemen and some of the local gentry as well. The musicians were tucked in a corner, so close together they could hardly move their arms. The long evening sun was glancing in through the stained-glass windows, shining on the Dudley coats of arms and pedigrees and giving a warm golden glow to everything.

The music struck up. We danced the first figure.

Then in came Sarah, with Mary arranging her train, and everyone kneeled to her—including the Queen herself! (Which made Carmina and Penelope giggle and almost spoiled the trick.)

As we paced through the next bit of the dance, which I knew, I watched the Queen out of the corner of my eye. She is a very good dancer, but she has something else which Sarah doesn't, and I don't know what it is. You just want to watch her and not anybody else.

When it came to the time for taking partners, there was Prince Sven, very gallantly offering the Queen of the May his hand and whirling her around him, while Sarah giggled that infectious laugh of hers.

I caught sight of the Earl of Leicester, who was watching her and frowning slightly. He shook his head, almost imperceptibly, then looked carefully at the rest of us Maids and Ladies-in-Waiting. I knew at once when he had finally spotted the Queen: his eyes rested on her, narrowed, and then he smiled.

He went up to her, bowed and offered her his hand. The Queen curtsied and took it and so they danced together, perfectly in tune, as if they were one person, dancing by themselves in an unimportant corner, with nobody but me bothering to watch.

Meanwhile, Prince Sven was showing off how well he could jump, and Sarah was being very impressed. Even when she's pretending to be the Queen she can't help being Sarah, can she?

The Queen and the Earl of Leicester saw how attentive Prince Sven was being to the false Queen of the May, and they looked at each other and smiled as they whirled in the figures of the dance.

When that part of the masque finished, I stood on a table to make my speech—I'm quite good at reciting, even when the poetry's terrible. I had just launched into it when I felt John watching me, and that made me pause for a moment—I don't know why, I just lost track of where I was. But then I caught myself and went on, *Eliza*'ing all over the place, until I saw someone waving from the back of the Hall, which distracted me again.

I stared for a moment, and realized it was Ellie. She was pointing at something, and then at her mouth and then at the Queen. I had no idea what she thought she was doing—she really shouldn't even have been there, for the household servants don't attend masques and bankets, except to hand round food and so on. She waved her arms even more when

I frowned in puzzlement, and as I had to concentrate to get the last bit of the speech right, I gave up trying to understand and looked away.

The end of my speech was all about the Bear with the Ragged Staff, which is the badge of the Earls of Warwick. Earl of Warwick is one of the titles the Queen has given to Robert Dudley, the Earl of Leicester. And my speech finished by my telling how the bear would gladly give his head to entertain and delight the Queen. I shouted it out, while the amazing marchpane and sugar-plate subtlety of the bear—which I had slightly damaged—was brought in on a shield by two serving men. Then two of the squires approached the bear with large knives, and cut off the whole head!

Inside were little wrapped gifts, which the squires started throwing to all the dryads and naiads. Lady Jane and Carmina had an unseemly scuffle over one package with a bracelet in it, hissing, "It's mine!" and, "No, it's mine! I saw it first!" like children.

I completely missed the one thrown at me, but someone picked it up for me and I saw that it was John, bowing and smiling as he handed it to me. "My lady, here is your trinket," he said.

And then I heard Ellie shouting, "My lady! My Lady Grace, 'ere—quick!"

Her voice sounded quite desperate, so I curtsied to John and, sighing, turned to where Ellie had managed to sidle round the room. She had her hand to her mouth and I wondered why. Then, as I made my way over to her, I saw that she was using a piece of scrap cloth to dab at a really nasty cut on her lip.

"What happened?" I asked. "Who hurt you?"

I couldn't hear her reply, because at that moment there was a big blast of music, and a choir of boys started to sing of how the stars would fall for shame in comparison with the beauty of the Queen of the May, the fair Eliza.

I drew closer. Ellie had something in her other hand—it looked like a bit of bark with something glittering in it.

"There's glass in the bear, broken glass . . . ," she said urgently.

For a moment I just stared stupidly. What was she saying? I looked at the thing she was waving, and suddenly realized it was the bear's ear from the subtlety—with Ellie's toothmarks in it—and, glittering in the middle, several shards of broken glass!

I felt my back and belly go icy-cold with horror. I picked it up to take a closer look. There was no mistake—long, sharp pieces of glass were poking out of the sugary almond mixture.

"Look! It's full of glass!" said Ellie, taking the cloth away from her mouth. "It really hurts. Stop the Queen from eating it. . . ."

The world seemed to slow down as I span round to look for the Queen. I stared across the Hall. There was Sarah, very graciously enthroned under her Cloth of Estate as the Queen of the May, with Prince Sven standing handsomely beside her. She was thoroughly enjoying herself, being Queen for a day, and she was laughing as the squires paraded towards her with the head of the bear. One of them used a fancy Italian fork to cut a slice from the subtlety and offer it to her—

I shouted, "Stop, don't eat it!"

But the choir was still singing. She couldn't hear a word. And she loves sweetmeats.

I picked up my skirts, satin leaves and streamers and all, and ran between all the servants, the courtiers, and the ladies, to where Lady Sarah sat happily, about to accept the forkful of marchpane.

"Stop!" I shouted again, as she took it from the fork.

A few people were turning now, but they were laughing, thinking this was part of the masque. So I threw myself at Sarah, nearly slipping on some silk flowers, and whacked the bit of marchpane out of her hand so that it flew across the room.

If I hadn't been a girl—and therefore not as much of a threat to the Queen as a man—I think I might have been killed! All the gentlemen of the Queen's Guard had their swords out to defend Her Majesty; all the courtiers and the Swedish gentlemen drew as well, and the nearest two gentlemen shouted and reached for me. I didn't want to blurt out why I had done it, though, because I felt sure the Queen would want to keep it quiet, just as she had all the other so-called accidents.

Sarah was staring at me, holding the hand I had whacked. And then, as I looked at her, an idea suddenly came to me. I put my hand to my forehead, said loudly, "Oh dear, I feel very dizzy!" and dropped to the floor in the dramatic swoon we had practised earlier.

Sarah leaned over in astonishment as I collapsed, and I whispered to her, "Don't eat the bear, it's got glass in it!" and then let my head fall back and shut my eyes.

I lay still, listening hard. First, I could hear all the swords being hastily put away, and then Mary, and someone else, wearing Sarah's kirtle—but oh, of course, it was the Queen, pretending to be Sarah—bent over me.

The Queen was now in a furious temper with me for making such a scene. "Your Majesty," she said to Sarah, in cold ringing tones that should have given the game away to anyone with half a brain. "I shall go with her and see if the cool air amends her humours."

"Thank you, Your, um, my lady," said Sarah, with as much dignity as she could muster.

Two of the gentlemen gripped hands, seated me on them, and carried me out of the Hall to the greensward outside, where they laid me down.

"She will be well enough," said the Queen. "Pray go back and join the dancing."

They went, because it would never occur to anyone not to do as she says, even when she's pretending to be ordinary.

"I know perfectly well there is nothing wrong with you, Grace," growled the Queen to me. "What in the Devil's name was all that mummery about? And incidentally, do not even *think* of joining a troupe of players, for you will starve in a month."

I opened my eyes and still couldn't see, so I rearranged my dryad's mask and sat up a bit. Mary

Shelton and the Queen were both looking at me quizzically.

"I had to do it, Your Majesty," I said. "There's broken glass in that marchpane subtlety and I had to stop poor Lady Sarah from biting into it."

"What?" exclaimed the Queen.

I showed her the bit of subtlety Ellie had showed me. In fact, in my mad dash across the Hall, I had gripped it so tightly I had cut myself on it.

The Queen took it from me and looked closely. "Good God!" she said. "How did you get this?"

"Um . . . it fell off the subtlety by accident, and my friend Ellie—"

"Never mind," whispered the Queen quickly. "It's enough that you found it out. And although I wasn't very impressed with your swoon, in the heat of the moment it was quite a clever thing to do. Now, Grace, you must find out who is doing these things and quickly, for tomorrow, before we leave, the Swedish Prince will ask if he may continue his suit. I shall therefore escort you to your chamber, and then I shall go back and explain that you are now resting, but that you were taken with a sudden megrim and thought there was a spider upon the sweetmeat. Meanwhile, you must find out the source of these outrages."

I was sad to miss the rest of the masque, but relieved that the Queen was trusting me to investigate further.

"Shall I stay with her?" asked Mary Shelton, who hadn't heard what the Queen had been saying.

"No, child," said the Queen patiently. "You must escort me back to the Hall. And I will tell Mrs. Champernowne that I feel Grace should rest alone until the masque ends." She then turned to me. "Use the time wisely, Grace."

I nodded. Mary Shelton helped me up and then she and the Queen escorted me up the spiral stairs to the Maids of Honour, our chamber.

When Mary and the disguised Queen had gone safely back to the Hall, I crept down the stairs to look for Ellie. I found her in the courtyard and explained what the Queen wanted me to do. Unfortunately, neither of us really knew where to start. We sat together in silence for a few minutes, thinking.

Suddenly, it occurred to me that John might be of help in finding out who had put the glass in the subtlety. After all, he had been around the Banqueting House when he found me inside—mayhap he had seen others coming and going from the tent also.

"Ellie," I said, "could you ask John Hull to come out and talk to me?"

She nodded and hurried into the Hall.

She seemed to be taking an awfully long time. While I waited, I wracked my brains to try and think who could be doing the mischief.

When Ellie came back, she was alone. "'E's not there," she said. "I looked carefully."

Perchance he had felt ill and gone back to his tent. All of the Earl of Leicester's attendants were camping near the lake, so that the Ladies-in-Waiting, the Maids of Honour, and the Privy Councillors, like Secretary Cecil, could sleep in the rooms in the castle and be near the Queen.

Ellie and I headed over to the little encampment by the lake to try and find John.

It was quite deserted, except for a pageboy, who was supposedly on watch to prevent any courtiers from thieving, but was in fact fast asleep, curled up by a fire.

I woke him up. "Do you know where John Hull is?" I asked, and he pointed at one of the outermost tents.

Ellie and I went over to it and cautiously peeped in through the flap. It was quite light in the tiny tent, for the moon was full, and I immediately saw that John was not within. The tent was rather smelly. Shirts and socks were lying in a terrible muddle.

Just as I turned away, a livery doublet caught my eye. It was poking out from beneath John's straw mattress, and in the moonlight that flooded the tent it looked as though it was in Sir William Cecil's colours.

I stared at it, my heart thundering. I could think of no reason at all why one of the Earl of Leicester's men would have a livery from Sir William Cecil.

Unless he wanted to take drugged ale to a fire-work master, and pretend it came from Cecil!

In a daze, I pulled out the doublet and the jerkin that was with it. Ellie and I stared at them—there was no mistake.

Something hard and heavy seemed to be bundled up in the livery. I unwrapped it, and found it was a chisel. I remembered that John had been politely looking after me in the maze—and then he had disappeared, just before the tail had fallen off the lion statue. And John had come in and found Ellie and me in the Banqueting House. Had *he* been in there previously, pushing glass into the softer part of the subtlety?

I wrapped the chisel up again and pushed the livery out of sight once more. Ellie and I came out of the tent and just looked at each other.

"Cor," said Ellie at last. "What do you want to do, Grace?"

But I still couldn't believe it. Could John have caused *all* those mysterious accidents? He had been near me when I mounted up to go on the hunt. But then he'd disappeared for a while.

I gulped. Perhaps that was why he had been paying court to me in the way he had—to give him an excuse for getting close to the Queen through me.

But why? Why on earth would he want to do such things? He was one of the Earl of Leicester's henchmen: why would he want to discredit his lord? It didn't make any sense. It couldn't be John because he didn't have any reason to cause false accidents.

Well, if it wasn't John, that livery was still evidence and I wanted it. "Can we take that doublet and jerkin up to the castle with us?" I asked Ellie.

Ellie frowned. "It's a bit obvious carrying Cecil's livery around . . . I know, I'll get a laundry bag to put it in and I'll carry it. Nobody will ask questions then."

So I stayed by the tent while Ellie ran over to the

laundrywomen's encampment, halfway round the lake.

I was just sitting in the shadow of the tent, twiddling my thumbs, when I heard people coming. It was some of the Swedish attendants, laughing and joking together as they walked between the tents. Then I saw John heading towards me, too. My heart pounded—what if he was coming to his tent? I froze, frantically wondering what to say if he saw me. It was going to be so embarrassing!

But he went straight into his tent, picked up a bottle, and left—passing about three feet from me. Thank the Lord, he didn't see me. I think my leafy dryad costume and mask must have made me look enough like a bush that he didn't notice I was there.

He passed the attendants—they were talking uproariously in Swedish and sounded quite drunk. One of them must have said something funny, because all the others laughed. And, to my surprise, John laughed, too!

I stared at him. He was looking at the attendants. And I realized that he was laughing at the same joke they were—which meant that he understood Swedish!

It was like ice-water down my back. For a while I

was so numb with shock I couldn't move. I just sat there, thinking, John understands Swedish. He sounds English, but he knows how to speak Swedish! And that means that he *could* be working for Prince Sven. It could have been John that collected Sir William Cecil's livery from the Wardrobe, and then wore it to deliver the drugged ale to Rosa's father. And it could have been John who disguised himself as a merman and scared Rosa away from the fireworks—and all to discredit the Earl of Leicester, for the sake of Prince Sven. It seemed incredible.

Moments later, I heard a rustle, and Ellie came out of the shadows holding her laundry bag. "What's wrong?" she asked at once.

I told her what I had just seen and heard and she whistled softly.

"I can't believe it," I said, with a very peculiar mixture of feelings in my stomach.

"It would make sense, though, wouldn't it?" said Ellie at last.

"Yes," I agreed miserably. "Yes, it would." Because if John were really working for Prince Sven, I realized, he would have reason to discredit the Earl of Leicester. If the Earl, famous for being the Queen's favourite, fell out of favour with Her

Majesty, then Prince Sven would have a far better chance of persuading the Queen to marry him!

I knew I would have to speak to the Queen as soon as I could, but first Ellie and I sneaked into the tent, took the jerkin and doublet and stuffed them into the bag Ellie had brought. Then Ellie carried it over her shoulder, muttering about how heavy it was.

We walked back to the castle in silence, while I desperately tried to think of another explanation for our discoveries. And then I remembered something else and stopped in my tracks: the day after the mysterious merman had caused a dreadful firework accident which injured little Gypsy Pete—John Hull had had a burn on his hand. He'd told me about it at the Banqueting House. He said he'd been burned by a poker while he was mulling ale for the Earl of Leicester—but mulled ale is something you drink in winter, when it's cold, not in blazing August!

Ellie was staring at me questioningly, but I shook my head and carried on to the courtyard. There were a few gentlemen there, taking the air. But then a new dance started, a Volta, and they all rushed inside.

Ellie and I crept up to one of the windows and climbed on a bench to see what was happening. There was the Queen of the May, still enthroned, chatting animatedly with Prince Sven, while Lady Helena translated with a highly amused expression on her face.

And there was the Queen herself, still dancing with the Earl of Leicester. The expression on his face made my heart melt, really it did, and I'm not a silly romantical creature like Lady Sarah. The Queen was dancing enthusiastically, her eyes behind her mask snapping and flashing in delight. But the Earl had no mask. He was holding up her hand as she did the footwork and his face simply looked happy—tender and happy. It made my eyes water and my nose itch, because it reminded me of the way my father had looked at my mother when he came home for the last time from the French War.

I coughed and wiped my nose on my sleeve. I can't think why I was so soft—except that I was thoroughly upset and not at all pleased to have solved the mystery. Even though I thought he must have been using me, I still didn't want to get John into trouble. Traitors have a terrible death—they're hanged, drawn, and quartered. And causing false accidents—probably so that the Queen would lose patience with the Earl of Leicester and look kindly on Prince Sven—well, it had to be traitorous, didn't it?

Prince Sven was looking a fool now, and he didn't

even know it, for there he was, busily courting one of the Queen's Maids of Honour, while the Queen whirled and stamped with his rival not three feet away.

The dance finished and the trumpets sounded. Sarah stood up on her dais, said a few words which I couldn't hear—for her voice is so light—and flung aside her mask.

Everyone gasped and laughed. Prince Sven's face was a picture of fury and thwarted hope. I saw his hand go to his sword hilt, before he stopped himself.

Sarah curtsied to the company and laughed prettily, then walked very gracefully down to where the Queen stood and kneeled to her, flinging out her arms to present the true Queen of Beauty.

The Queen took off her own mask and there was another gasp. Everybody went to one knee, including the Earl of Leicester. I could hear her words clearly, as she declared in ringing tones, "My thanks to all who played this pretty jest upon you, and my thanks to all of you for being taken in by it!" She smiled in quite a spiteful way at Prince Sven, as she went on, "Oft-times our true selves are best known by trickery, when one who claims to love cannot tell the difference, and another knows at once the true from the false." At this, she smiled down at the Earl of Leicester, who was gazing admiringly at her. Finally she said waspishly to the Prince, "Alas, Your Grace, had you been more discerning of eye, who knows what might have happened?"

The Prince listened to the translation—given by Eric, his secretary, who was at his side by then. Eric was looking even more miserable than usual, and the Prince's face was a mask of fury. "A pretty trick, Your Majesty," he said through Eric. "A child's play for a summer's masque. My gentlemen and I vill now return to our tents."

And off they all went, which was extremely rude, since they should have waited for the Queen and her ladies to leave first.

Ellie and I ran as fast as we could to the main keep of the castle and up the stairs to the Maids of Honour, our chamber. I leaped into bed and Ellie hid the bag of livery underneath and then bustled about the room tidying up.

Now the girls have come clattering up the stairs, still talking and laughing, and Lady Sarah is looking flushed and happy after her triumph as Queen of the May. In a moment I will go and seek an audience with the Queen.

I am back in the Maids of Honour, our chamber, and worried about John and what will happen to him when the Queen's Guard catch him.

The Queen was not pleased by my news, but she was relieved that we at last seem to be nearing the truth. She called the Earl of Leicester in, since John was one of his henchmen.

I told the Queen and the Earl everything I had worked out. I had brought Ellie with me as a witness—and she had the stolen livery. Ellie showed the livery to Her Majesty.

"Please, Your Majesty," I got out, my words stumbling over one another. "Please don't be too hard on John. I don't think he meant to kill anyone. . . ."

"He's young and very foolish," said the Queen. "I take no revenge on servants if I can. But it may be unavoidable. My lord Earl?"

"We shall have to see," said the Earl, looking angry indeed. "But I will take revenge no further if he has been acting for Prince Sven, and if he now truthfully turns Queen's Evidence and tells us all the Prince intended."

The Earl talked to three of the Gentlemen of the Guard, who immediately headed for the encampment of the Earl's attendants by the lakeside.

I didn't want to see John arrested or questioned, so I left the livery where it was and kneeled to the Queen. "May I go to my bed now, Your Majesty?" I asked sadly. "I had rather not humiliate him by being here when you—"

"Of course," said the Queen gently. "And be not too sad about John, for he did most certainly take advantage of your kind nature. Nor did you stint your duty to tell us when you knew it was him."

"Yes, Your Majesty," I said, and went out of her chamber with Ellie, and back into the Maids' chamber, where they were leaping about the beds in their smocks having a pillow fight and shrieking.

And I'm afraid I don't want to join in, even though the pillows are flying, and so are the cushions, and one of the lapdogs is barking now. . . .

A short time later

I'm writing this because I can't go to sleep, and I have no pillow, and the air is full of feathers, which make me sneeze.

In the end I joined in the pillow fight, because someone knocked my book sideways and made a great long blot on it, so I had to take revenge on them. And in fact I forgot all about John because as I swept wildly with my pillow, I caught it on a carving on the bed and the pillow ripped—and then the room was full of a snowstorm of feathers, at which the lapdogs started leaping about and barking and trying to catch the feathers and sneezing.

"What, in the name of God, is all this racket?" roared a voice, and we all stopped and turned to stare, then dropped to our knees because it was the Queen in her dressing gown looking extremely annoyed.

"Um . . . very sorry, Your Majesty . . . ," faltered Mary Shelton.

"Sorry . . . ," we all muttered shamefacedly.

"Some of us are trying to sleep!" exclaimed the Queen. "I will write to your parents and send every one of you home in disgrace, if I do not this instant have peace so I may rest. Do you understand?"

"Yes, Your Majesty," we chorused.

As she turned to go, she caught my eye and gave a little jerk of her head. "Grace, you may go and fetch me a cup of wine to settle my stomach," she said.

So I put my own dressing gown on, and ran downstairs to the small sideboard where the extra wine flagon is kept, and brought it back upstairs and panted into the Queen's own chamber with it. Lady Helena was there, fast asleep in the truckle bed ready to attend the Queen. So Her Majesty hadn't really needed to send me.

"Here you are, Your Majesty," I said, going to one knee. "I'm really so sorry—"

"Oh, hush, child," interrupted the Queen. "I don't *really* mind one pillow fight! But I'm afraid that none of my gentlemen has been able to find John anywhere. I have sent riders out along the roads, and we will use the dogs in the morning, but it seems he may have got away." She looked at me very seriously. "Now, are you sure that you did not warn him, Grace?"

"No, of course I didn't!" I cried. "I would never do that. I never even thought of it. Once I knew what he was up to, I came straight to Your Majesty."

"What might have alerted him?" the Queen asked.

"Well, I suppose he may have found that Sir William Cecil's livery was missing from under his palliasse? I'm sorry, I didn't think that—"

"Ah. I expect it was that," agreed the Queen. "It's a pity. Unless we can catch him, I cannot possibly tax His Grace the Prince with his outrages against me. But no matter—the Prince is embarrassed already, for other reasons, and so he should be."

I nodded. "My lord the Earl of Leicester saw through your disguise in about two heartbeats," I remarked.

The Queen smiled. "Of course he did," she said. "My Robin is very sharp-eyed. Well, we shall see what we shall see in the morning."

And so I left Her Majesty and returned to my chamber. And I know I shouldn't, but I do hope John got away. Perhaps he should have stayed to explain himself, but if he ran away, I hope he escapes. I don't want to see his severed head above London Bridge.

Late in the morning

We are in the middle of packing up again, but mine is finished and it is much more important that I write down all that has happened.

First of all this morning, when we were all dressed in our travelling habits, the Queen decided she would have a final ride around the lake, with the Earl and Prince Sven. Lady Helena and the other Ladies-in-Waiting accompanied her.

I had packed up quite early, because of not being able to sleep properly, and Ellie had helped me. So while the other Maids of Honour were still arguing over who had hidden the pot of crimson wax, and whose was this smock with the grass-smeared back, I crept out of the keep with Ellie.

We wandered along the road that wound down past the paddock where the Prince's carts were lined up. The paddock was in an uproar as the Swedish Prince broke camp. All his men were taking down the pavilions, and the servants were staggering about under long tent poles, putting them in the row of carts lent by the Queen.

The carthorses were having their breakfast in their nosebags and stamping their soup-plate feet.

I overheard one of the carters saying, "They foreign gents don't know how to stow a cart properly," to the crowd of children and dogs who had come up from the village to watch everyone leaving.

As we sauntered along beside the carts, patting the horses, we came upon Masou standing thoughtfully on his hands next to an apple tree. "Masou, you're back," I cried.

He flexed his arms, jumped down smoothly onto his feet, and came over to us, smiling. "Back?" he said, blinking in a puzzled way.

"From being Puck—we've 'ardly seen you," sniffed Ellie.

Masou grinned. "I'm glad I'm back, too," he admitted. "It was a lot of work. And I've been looking after Gypsy Pete. He's feeling better already."

Ellie and I smiled to hear that the little boy was on the mend. Then the three of us walked along the row of carts, peering inside to see what Prince Sven had brought from Sweden to make him feel at home.

Suddenly, I noticed something odd. Among the loaded carts, there was one packed with carpets and rugs and tapestries and so on, all rolled up. There was no food on board at all, and yet every dog in the place was gathered around it, sniffing with interest at the wheels. One of the big lymers even put his huge paws on the side of the cart and pushed his nose in amongst the hangings. . . .

"Masou," I hissed, "give me a boost!" And I hurried towards the cart while the coast was clear—the carter was having a pork pie for his own breakfast, while his horse munched and whuffled in his nosebag.

Masou followed me, linked his hands, and boosted me up into the cart. I looked among the hangings, while the curious lymer tried to follow—so Masou caught his collar and pulled him down.

There certainly was a peculiar smell on the cart. I pulled at a rolled-up tapestry, and it unrolled slightly—revealing a leg! A stiff, dead leg, side by side with another.

Feeling sick, I pushed it open further, and saw John's hose, and the hand with the burn on it, clenched tightly shut. I touched it once. It was quite still and cold.

I jumped down at once and moved away from the cart, shaking.

"What is it, Grace?" asked Ellie, catching my hands. "You look white as your shift."

I am not Lady Sarah, and I am *not* going to swoon, I told myself angrily. For I was very angry indeed. There had been nothing at all wrong with John the night before, when I saw him fetch a bottle from his tent. "There's a c-corpse in the cart," I gasped. "It's John."

"Oh, my God," said Ellie. "Are you sure?"

Masou had already jumped up and lifted the tapestry. He jumped down again, not pale, but certainly looking shocked. He nodded once at Ellie.

"I have to tell the Queen," I said. "But if we show we're suspicious, the Prince will simply leave the rest of his equipment here and depart at once."

"I'd say the carts are nearly ready to go anyway," Ellie pointed out. "I should think they will go first, and the Prince and his gentlemen will leave once they get back from the ride with the Queen. That's how they usually do it, because the carts go so slowly."

"We must stop them, and we must get the Queen to have her Gentlemen of the Guard search the carts," Masou said.

"No," I said, "that won't work. He's a Sovereign Prince. The Queen can't just search his carts, there'd be a diplomatic incident."

Masou and Ellie were staring at me.

I thought frantically and came up with an idea. "We've got to do something to make the cart tip so that everything falls off," I said. "If you two distract the carter so he doesn't hear me, I'll creep up and knock the pin out of the wheel axle."

"Distract 'im?" said Ellie thoughtfully.

"I know," put in Masou. "We'll fight."

They crept away, with Masou whispering into Ellie's ear. Soon they were on the other side of the road, in the paddock, and Masou was shouting at Ellie very realistically.

"You evil kinchin mort!" he yelled, which is thieves' cant for a girl (which I didn't know he knew). "You prigged my best jerkin, you know you did."

"No, I never!" shrieked Ellie. "You lost it and you're just trying to get me in trouble!"

"You did!" roared Masou. "Give it back!"

"I never!" shrieked Ellie again, and aimed a great slap at him.

They were very clever—Masou fell back, clapping his hands to make it sound as if she'd hit him, and then he slapped her and she did the same. And then they were acting the most wonderful fight. Of course, the carters soon gathered round and started laying bets.

I hefted a stone in my hand and crept up to the back wheel of the cart that had John on it. There was the pin. I looked at it carefully. It went right through the axle, holding the wheel on so that it could still turn. There was a cap on one end, which I took off with my fingers, as the shrieking and swearing from Ellie and Masou got louder and louder. There was a roar—ah, I knew they must be grappling now.

My hands were sweating. I tapped the end of the pin with the stone, but it was stuck. I tapped it again, harder, and it popped out and fell on the floor. Quickly, I picked it up and replaced it with a stick, so it would not be obvious the pin was out. I hoped that the minute the cart went over a rut or a stone, its wheel would fall off and everything in the cart would be tipped into the road. Then I slipped away, and as soon as Ellie and Masou saw that I was finished, Ellie dead-legged Masou and took to her heels up to the castle, with Masou chasing her.

I went up the path much more sedately, until I was out of sight of the paddock. Then I ran after Ellie and Masou. I found them in the corner of the stable yard, where they had collapsed breathlessly, laughing at their play-fight.

I realized I needed a plan to reveal what the Prince had done, and to prevent him from leaving with his crimes undiscovered. So I thought very carefully about what to do, and decided it must be dramatic.

When Masou and Ellie had recovered, I asked them to help me find a dryad disguise and mask, and get all dressed up—so no one could recognize me. Then I found a nice spreading chestnut tree on the Queen's route back to the castle, and got Masou to give me a boost again. I am very good at tree-climbing, although Mrs. Champernowne thinks it disgraceful.

Masou and Ellie hid in the bushes, while I settled down to wait for the Queen's party.

Sure enough, after about ten minutes I heard hooves approaching. The Queen rode into sight, surrounded by the Earl of Leicester, Prince Sven, and all the attendants.

Feeling very nervous now that the time was upon me, I stood up on my branch and steadied myself on another one. "Halt!" I cried.

Most of the party thought that this was another of the Earl's entertainments, but I think the Queen recognized my voice, for she frowned as soon as I began my speech.

"Here's a story I'll relate, of Elizabeth, the Queen so great . . . ," I started, and then gave up the verse because it's much harder to do than it looks. You try to think of a rhyme for Elizabeth!

"Pray listen, Great Queen," I began again. "A sad tale I have to tell. . . ." And I related the whole chain of events—all about the Swedish Prince's plan, and how it had failed.

As I told my story, there were many gasps of amazement from the Queen's Ladies-in-Waiting and the Earl of Leicester's henchmen. Eric, the Prince's secretary, had come forward to translate for his lord. And Prince Sven looked more and more furious—

until I was glad to be out of reach in my tree, and not down on the ground.

At one point, he made a move to leave, but somehow there were too many of the Earl's attendants in his way. "O beauteous Queen—" he started to say, but she held up her hand imperiously to hush him.

I gripped the branch tighter, took a breath, and carried on with my tale. When I got to the point where I suspected John had discovered Secretary Cecil's livery missing from his tent, Prince Sven suddenly spurred his horse forward, shoving one of the Earl's henchmen out of the way. "I vill not listen to more childish rubbish," he snarled. "Ve go now. Good day, Your Majesty."

Followed by his attendants, Prince Sven rode towards his carts and waved the drivers on angrily. They whipped up the horses and set off. First one cart, then another.

The one with John's body on it started off. It was rolling along perfectly well. Oh, no! I thought. Had they noticed and replaced the pin? Was my speech for nothing?

The cart went over a big pothole. Very slowly, the wheel rolled up, came off the end of the axle, and fell over on its side. As it did so, that side of the cart tilted and tipped, until all the carpets and rugs and tapestries tumbled off and onto the ground. And there in the middle of them all, its stiff limbs sticking out at odd angles, lay John's body!

There was a huge gasp from everyone watching. The dogs barked joyfully, and the lymer made a dive for one of the corpse's legs. Luckily, the carter was quick-thinking, and he stood on the seat and cracked his whip to keep the dogs away.

There was a moment of absolute silence.

Then came the Queen's voice. "Your Grace," she said coldly. "What is that?"

Prince Sven gabbled something, but Eric, his translator, wasn't doing his job. The tall, grim-looking man had suddenly hidden his face in his hands and hunched forward over his horse's neck.

"Well, Your Grace?" snapped the Queen.

Lady Helena came forward, offering to help with the translating. Her lovely face was white and strained.

Eric straightened up decisively, dismounted, went over to the Queen, and kneeled before her. "Your Majesty," he said, "I throw myself on your mercy."

"Yes?"

"Johan, he is . . . he vas my brother," he said, gesturing at the body. "My father married again ven my mother died of plague. He married an

175

Englishwoman. Her son vas Johan. He learned English as vell as Swedish, much better than me. His Grace, the Prince, sent him ahead to become part of the Earl of Leicester's household and then—to do as this maid has said—to make accidents against the Queen to frighten her and make the Earl look careless."

The Prince snarled something vicious at Eric, who ignored him. Lady Helena whispered a quick translation to the Queen, who looked furious.

"Hold hard, Your Grace," she coldly. "This is my realm, not yours. I will not have you threaten anyone in it."

Prince Sven's lip curled with contempt.

"I vas against it, but I came with my Prince," Eric carried on. "Johan vas young and eager, he wanted to be an Earl—which the Prince promised when he should be King Consort."

The Queen sniffed very loudly at that.

"And then, ven Johan realized he had been discovered, he must have gone to his Prince, Your Grace, and asked for help. And vat did you do?" Eric's voice shook with emotion and he pointed at the Prince. "You killed him. And then you hid his body with your hangings, to throw him in a hedge ven you vere out of sight of the Court. This I vill not have."

Prince Sven shouted at him in Swedish and Eric shouted back. Prince Sven drew his sword, at which every one of the gentlemen present also drew their swords—and the Earl of Leicester immediately moved his horse between the Queen and the Prince, so she had to peer around him.

"Mr. Hatton," she called to the Captain of the Guard, "arrest that man." She was pointing at Eric.

Hatton came forward and placed Eric under arrest. Eric looked as if he didn't really care—he was just staring at the Prince with his face full of hatred.

Prince Sven snapped something in Swedish to the Queen, which Lady Helena translated.

"Give him to you?" repeated the Queen incredulously, with Lady Helena's mellifluous voice quietly translating after her. "Give anyone to a murderer? Oh, no, Your Grace, you mistake me. I have arrested him to keep him safe from you. He will stand trial in an English court, but as he has already turned Queen's Evidence, I think he will not be too greatly condemned. We will also take the trouble to bury decently your secret servant, John Hull, which it seems you could not."

More Swedish from the Prince.

"Your suit to us is at an end," said the Queen with quiet venom. "We are well aware that we cannot arrest or try you, no matter how appalling your crime. And appalling it is. You have recklessly caused a child to be injured—a *child,* Your Grace—and now this poor young man has been murdered on your orders. Your antics have offended us. We prefer your room to your presence. Please return to the nearest seaport and take the first ship to Stockholm. I shall be writing to your royal father with a full report of your doings here. You have a week to quit our realm."

The Prince had the wit to say nothing, perhaps because most of the English gentlemen still had their swords at the ready. He sheathed his blade at last, turned his horse, and moved off, without the slightest bow or courtesy to the Queen. After a moment's hesitation, his gentlemen followed him.

"A very ill-mannered knave," the Queen said loudly, taking a deep breath. "Now, will you please come down from that tree?" she said to me.

⁓

Once the Queen had seen me safely down from the tree, she ordered everyone to move on before they could recognize me. I was quite shaky from all the strain, but Masou and Ellie came out from their hiding place to help me, and soon I was back in my usual apparel and a perfectly ordinary Maid of Honour once again.

As I got back to our chamber, Mrs. Champernowne waylaid me. "Where have you been, Lady Grace? The Queen commands that you attend her in the garden. Get along with you now, and don't keep Her Majesty waiting," she said, in her sing-song Welsh accent.

I hurried to find the Queen. She was sitting in a bower with the Earl of Leicester near her. He stared at me as if I had two heads, which made me nervous. The Queen had clearly told him that it had been me in the tree.

I explained how I had discovered John's body— and what I had done to the wheel of the cart—and the Queen listened with her head cocked on one side. When I finished with climbing the tree, she smiled. "I am very pleased with you, Grace, and with your efforts," she said, "though I feel that climbing a tree like a tumbler is rather too danger- ous for a Maid of Honour. Please do not take such risks in future."

I looked at the ground in embarrassment.

The Queen went on. "I have already righted some of the wrongs that John Hull caused," she told me. And I confess I had to blink back tears at the men- tion of his name, because it grieves me to think that such a nice young man, with such lively blue eyes, should have wound up dead in a cart for trying to help his lord.

I realized the Queen was still talking and forced myself to concentrate on what she was saying. "Sam Ledbury is returned to his proper duties in the stable, though never have we had a tidier dungheap!" she remarked. "And Master Herron, the firework master, has been paid, and he shall have more work at the Accession Day Tilts." She paused, turned to the Earl of Leicester and whispered in his ear. The Earl bowed and moved away towards the stables.

The Queen held out her hand and took mine in hers. "I am sorry that your friendship with young John should end so sadly," she said softly. "And sorry that he should have been led into such wrong-doing, when he was not, I think, bad at heart. But do not be downcast, Grace. Not all young men have such poor manners as to be traitors in very truth."

I smiled back at her. "At least there will be no more deliberate accidents," I said. "And you will not marry the Swedish Prince and break my lord the Earl's heart."

"Do you think I would break his heart?" the Queen asked wistfully.

"Oh, yes, Your Majesty—you should have seen

how he was looking at you when you danced in disguise at the masque."

She paused for a long time before she spoke again, and I could hardly hear her voice or see her expression, for her face was turned away and shadowed by the bower. "I did see," she said quietly.

Then the Queen shook herself, smiled, and stood, smoothing out her skirts. At her gesture, I picked up her train and followed her out of the garden.

"Another successful discovery of miscreants and ill-doers by my Lady Pursuivant," said the Queen, smiling at me again. "Whatever did I do before I had you to investigate for me, Grace?"

Usually, nothing makes me happier than when the Queen praises me, but I was feeling miserable and somehow even her kind words could not lift my spirits—especially as she then sent me straight back to the Maids' chamber to help the others pack, since I had finished my own.

I hurried up the stairs to find that the men of the Removing Wardrobe were there, waiting for all the chests and boxes, while Lady Sarah and Lady Jane argued over whose fault it was neither of them had a complete pair of riding boots. Carmina was looking for a hat she had lost, and I helped Olwen and Ellie, by sitting on Lady Sarah's chest of clothes to make it shut.

Ellie was very kind and kept offering to bring me things—I think she could see how unhappy I was feeling. It saddens me that John came to such a sorry end, and I feel it will be some time before I am quite restored to my usual spirits. But I am glad that at least Her Majesty did not think John was entirely wicked. I wish he hadn't been using me, though. . . .

It is most surprising!

Lady Sarah just came over to whisper to me. "I'm so sorry about John," she hissed. "Even though he was a traitor, I'm sure he liked you really. He carried you all the way up the stairs, didn't he?"

I smiled gratefully at her because I did not really know what to say—it is very unlike Sarah to be so thoughtful, and her words cheered me greatly. I am very pleased that *she* thinks John was not just using me, for she knows a thing or two about young gentlemen.

And now I must put my daybooke away in my embroidery bag. We are going to the next great house, where there will be hardly any entertainments and no speeches—which is *such* a relief.

Army Virtuous, Barque Perilous, Black Knight of Melancholy, and *Giant Melancholy* are all names, invented by the writer, for the masque taking place as part of the Earl of Leicester's entertainments for the Queen. These are the kinds of names that would have been used in plays and masques of the time. The fancy names were inspired by the hugely popular romantic novels of the period. These stories usually featured knights in armor rescuing damsels in distress. So the names and terms used in *Conspiracy* are basically poetic names for characters and things in the play. Thus the Black Knight of Melancholy would have simply been a sad knight who always wore black, the Barque Perilous would have been a dangerous ship, etc.

ambler—a horse that moves along very slowly
aqua vitae—brandy

Arcadia—a paradisal location often featured in Greek pastoral poetry

banket—an alternative word for a banquet

battledore—a light flat bat or racquet

Bedlam—the major asylum for the insane in London during Elizabethan times—the name came from Bethlehem Hospital

Bergomask—a rustic dance

biggin cap—a child's hat

bodice—the top part of a woman's dress

brocade—a rich, gold-embroidered fabric

bum—bottom

cant—slang

caparison—decorative trappings for a horse

cavalcade—a procession on horseback

Chamberer—a servant of the Queen who cleaned her chamber for her—which the Maids of Honour and Ladies-in-Waiting, of course, could not be expected to do

Cloth of Estate—a kind of awning that went over the Queen's chair to indicate that she was the Queen

cloth of silver/gold—cloth woven from silk thread that had been wrapped in fine gold or silver wire

comfrey—an herb

coppice—a thicket of trees, or a copse

damask—a beautiful, self-patterned silk cloth woven

in Flanders. It originally came from Damascus—
hence the name.

daybooke—a book in which you would record your
sins each day so that you could pray about them.
The idea of keeping a diary or journal grew out of
this. Grace is using hers as a journal.

distempered—disordered, deranged

doublet—a close-fitting padded jacket worn by men

dryad—a wood nymph

en plein air—out of doors

falling-band collar—an ordinary collar as opposed to a
fancy one. In fact, the ordinary shirt collars seen
today are falling-band collars.

Farandole Snail Shell—a movement in a particular
French dance known as the Farandole

faun—a half-goat, half-man deity of the fields in classical mythology

fire pot—a clay pot, filled with material that would
easily catch fire, used to carry hot coals

fletching—the feathers on an arrow

forepart—the part of a garment that covers the chest

French War—the ongoing religious war between the
Catholics and the Protestants in France. Occasionally, the English got involved in the fighting
for political reasons.

Galliard—a sixteenth-century dance

harbinger—somebody who went ahead to announce the monarch

heal-all—a medicinal plant

henchman—a young serving man, often related to the person he was serving. His work might well involve bodyguard duties.

hose—tight-fitting cloth trousers worn by men

house-poet—a poet who lived in a noble's house and wrote poetry for him. Many nobles chose to support poets and playwrights on their staff as a way of showing off their wealth.

in earnest of—to show the sincerity of

jerkin—a close-fitting, hip-length, usually sleeveless jacket

kirtle—the skirt section of an Elizabethan dress

kissing-comfit—a spice, such as caraway, fennel, or aniseed, which was covered in sugar and eaten to make one's breath smell pleasant

Lady-in-Waiting—one of the ladies who helped to look after the Queen and kept her company

laudanum—an opium tincture in alcohol used to aid sleep

lymer—a bloodhound

madrigals—beautiful part-songs, which were very fashionable

Maid of Honour—a younger girl who helped to look after the Queen like a Lady-in-Waiting

manchet rolls—whole white bread

marchpane subtlety—a sculpture made out of marzipan and then colored

marmelada—a very thick jammy sweet often made from quinces

Mary Shelton—one of Queen Elizabeth's Maids of Honour (a Maid of Honour of this name really did exist; see below). Most Maids of Honour were not officially "ladies" (like Lady Grace), but they had to be of born of gentry.

masque—a masquerade, a masked ball

mead—an alcoholic drink made with honey

megrim—a migraine headache

mumming—acting

naiad—a water nymph

on progress—a term used when the Queen was touring parts of her realm. It was a kind of summer holiday for her.

Ordnancer—a supplier of military equipment, particularly firearms

palfrey—a horse ridden for pleasure, rather than into battle

palliasse—a thin mattress

parlour—a room off the hall that was just beginning to be used for eating, among other things

penner—a small leather case that could be attached to a belt. It was used for holding quills, ink, knife, and any other equipment needed for writing.

pillion seat—a saddle for a woman that included a soft cushion

plague—a virulent disease that killed thousands

posset—a hot drink made from sweetened and spiced milk curdled with ale or wine

prigged—stole

Puck—a mischievous spirit

pursuivant—one who pursues someone else

Queen's favour—an item of the Queen's, worn to show that she favored the wearer to win a contest

Queen's Guard—these were more commonly known as the Gentlemen Pensioners—young noblemen who guarded the Queen from physical attacks

sarsenet—Asian thin silk

Secretary Cecil—William Cecil, an administrator for the Queen (later made Lord Burghley)

shawm—a wind instrument

shift—a polite name for a smock

smock—a neck-to-ankles linen shirt worn by women

stays—the boned, laced bodice worn around the body under the clothes. Victorians called it a corset.

stews—public baths

sugar plate—sugar candy that could be molded like modeling clay, then dried and colored

sward, greensward—lawn, grass-covered soil

sweetmeats—sweets

taffety—taffeta fabric

ten-day-old urine—ten-day-old urine was used in the laundry for removing stubborn stains!

tertian fever—a fever that recurred every third day

tester—the frame of the bed canopy

tilting plate—armor worn for jousting

Tilting Yard—an area where knights in armor would joust, or tilt (i.e., ride at each other on horseback with lances)

tiring woman—a woman who helped a lady to dress

truckle bed—a small bed on wheels stored under the main bed

tumbler—an acrobat

unguent—a salve or ointment

veney—a bout or round of sword-fighting

Volta—a sixteenth-century dance very popular with Queen Elizabeth I

Every summer Queen Elizabeth I went on progress—a sort of summer vacation for the Court combined with a royal "walkabout." She would set off in mid-July and the progress would continue until mid-September. During this time, the Privy Counselors would follow the Queen around, meeting her as and when they could.

One reason for the progress was to keep the Queen and most of the Court out of London during the worst months of plague. It was also the only chance most of Elizabeth's subjects had of seeing their Queen at all—no TV, remember, no *People* magazine, and no photographs, either.

The Queen would stay with her noblemen, riding in procession from one big country mansion to another, stopping at the houses of lesser gentlemen to eat on the way. With her would go most of the

Court and their baggage train—consisting of about three hundred carts! It would take almost the whole day for the procession to pass through one place.

Playing host to the Queen was a great honor—some of her courtiers nearly bankrupted themselves in their attempts to build houses big enough to support the Queen's entourage and to provide suitable entertainments. However, others were less eager. There was supposedly one gentleman who, on hearing that the Queen planned to visit him, shut up his house and left the county so she couldn't!

Although the Queen saved money by eating at the expense of her lucky hosts, she spent about £2000 more than she saved, on transport costs—especially if she changed her mind about where she wanted to go on the morning she was due to leave, which she very often did.

In 1485, Queen Elizabeth I's grandfather, Henry Tudor, won the battle of Bosworth Field against Richard III and took the throne of England. He was known as Henry VII. He had two sons, Arthur and Henry. Arthur died while still a boy, so when Henry VII died in 1509, Elizabeth's father came to the throne and England got an eighth king called Henry—the notorious one who had six wives.

Wife number one—Catherine of Aragon—gave Henry one daughter called Mary (who was brought up as a Catholic) but no living sons. To Henry VIII this was a disaster, because nobody believed a queen could ever govern England. He needed a male heir.

Henry wanted to divorce Catherine so he could marry his pregnant mistress, Anne Boleyn. The Pope, the head of the Catholic Church, wouldn't allow him to annul his marriage, so Henry broke with the Catholic Church and set up the Protestant Church of England—or the Episcopal Church, as it's known in the United States.

Wife number two—Anne Boleyn—gave Henry another daughter, Elizabeth (who was brought up as a Protestant). When Anne then miscarried a baby boy, Henry decided he'd better get somebody new, so he accused Anne of infidelity and had her executed.

Wife number three—Jane Seymour—gave Henry a son called Edward and died of childbed fever a couple of weeks later.

Wife number four—Anne of Cleves—had no children. It was a diplomatic marriage and Henry didn't fancy her, so she agreed to a divorce (wouldn't you?).

Wife number five—Catherine Howard—had no children, either. Like Anne Boleyn, she was accused of infidelity and executed.

Wife number six—Catherine Parr—also had no children. She did manage to outlive Henry, though, but only by the skin of her teeth. Nice guy, eh?

Henry VIII died in 1547, and in accordance with the rules of primogeniture (whereby the firstborn son inherits from his father), the person who succeeded him was the boy Edward. He became

Edward VI. He was strongly Protestant but died young, in 1553.

Next came Catherine of Aragon's daughter, Mary, who became Mary I, known as Bloody Mary. She was strongly Catholic, married Philip II of Spain in a diplomatic match, but died childless five years later. She also burned a lot of Protestants for the good of their souls.

Finally, in 1558, Elizabeth came to the throne. She reigned until her death in 1603. She played the marriage game—that is, she kept a lot of important and influential men hanging on in hopes of marrying her—for a long time. At one time it looked as if she would marry her favorite, Robert Dudley, Earl of Leicester. She didn't, though, and I think she probably never intended to get married—would you, if you'd had a dad like hers? So she never had any children.

She was an extraordinary and brilliant woman, and during her reign, England first started to become important as a world power. Sir Francis Drake sailed round the world—raiding the Spanish colonies of South America for loot as he went. And one of Elizabeth's favorite courtiers, Sir Walter Raleigh, tried to plant the first English colony in North

America—at the site of Roanoke in 1585. It failed, but the idea stuck.

The Spanish King Philip II tried to conquer England in 1588. He sent a huge fleet of 150 ships, known as the Invincible Armada, to do it. It failed miserably—defeated by Drake at the head of the English fleet—and most of the ships were wrecked trying to sail home. There were many other great Elizabethans, too—including William Shakespeare and Christopher Marlowe.

After her death, Elizabeth was succeeded by James VI of Scotland, who became James I of England and Scotland. He was almost the last eligible person available! He was the son of Mary, Queen of Scots, who was Elizabeth's cousin, via Henry VIII's sister.

James's son was Charles I—the king who was beheaded after losing the English Civil War.

—

The stories about Lady Grace Cavendish are set in the year 1569, when Elizabeth was almost thirty-six and still playing the marriage game for all she was worth. The Ladies-in-Waiting and Maids of Honor at her Court weren't servants—they were companions and friends, supplied from upper-class families.

Not all of them were officially "ladies"—only those with titled husbands or fathers; in fact, many of them were unmarried younger daughters sent to Court to find themselves a nice rich lord to marry.

All the Lady Grace Mysteries are invented, but some of the characters in the stories are real people—Queen Elizabeth herself, of course, and Mrs. Champernowne and Mary Shelton as well. There never was a Lady Grace Cavendish (as far as we know!)—but there were plenty of girls like her at Elizabeth's Court. The real Mary Shelton foolishly made fun of the Queen herself on one occasion—and got slapped in the face by Elizabeth for her trouble! But most of the time, the Queen seems to have been protective of and kind to her Maids of Honor. She was very strict about boyfriends, though. There was one simple rule for boyfriends in those days: you couldn't have one. No boyfriends at all. You would get married to a person your parents chose for you and that was that. Of course, the girls often had other ideas!

Later on in her reign, the Queen had a full-scale secret service run by her great spymaster, Sir Francis Walsingham. His men, who hunted down priests and assassins, were called Pursuivants. There are also tantalizing hints that Elizabeth may have had her own personal sources of information—she certainly was very well informed, even when her counselors tried to keep her in the dark. And who knows whom she might have recruited to find things out for her? There may even have been a Lady Grace Cavendish, after all!

Don't miss

the first two

Lady Grace Mysteries,

ASSASSIN

and

BETRAYAL